GRADE
4

P9-DGZ-649

50¢

FRIENDS FOREVER

T.M.

THE BABY-SITTERS CLUB

THE MOVIE

FRIENDS FOREVER

BSC
THE BABY-SITTERS CLUB
T.M.

THE MOVIE

A novelization by A. L. Singer
From the movie written by Dalene Young
Based on the best-selling series by Ann M. Martin

SCHOLASTIC INC.
New York Toronto London Auckland Sydney

FRIENDS FOREVER

THE MOVIE

BEACON AND COLUMBIA PICTURES PRESENT
A SCHOLASTIC PRODUCTION "THE BABY-SITTERS CLUB" MUSIC BY DAVID MICHAEL FRANK
EXECUTIVE PRODUCERS MARC ABRAHAM, THOMAS A. BLISS, MARTIN KELTZ, DEBORAH FORTE BASED ON THE BOOK SERIES BY ANN M. MARTIN
WRITTEN BY DALENE YOUNG PRODUCED BY JANE STARTZ AND PETER O. ALMOND DIRECTED BY MELANIE MAYRON
DISTRIBUTED THROUGH SONY PICTURES RELEASING

If you purchased this book without a cover, you should be aware that this book is stolen property. It was reported as "unsold and destroyed" to the publisher, and neither the author nor the publisher has received any payment for this "stripped book."

No part of this publication may be reproduced in whole or in part, or stored in a retrieval system, or transmitted in any form or by any means, electronic, mechanical, photocopying, recording, or otherwise, without written permission of the publisher. For information regarding permission, write to Scholastic Inc., 555 Broadway, New York, NY 10012.

ISBN 0-590-60404-X

Text copyright © 1995 by Scholastic Inc.
Photographs copyright © 1995 by   Columbia Pictures Industries, Inc.
The Baby-sitters Club Movie © 1995   Beacon Communications Corp.
and Columbia Pictures Industries, Inc.
All rights reserved. Published by Scholastic Inc. THE BABY-SITTERS CLUB is a registered trademark of Scholastic Inc.

12 11 10 9 8 7 6 5 4 3 2 1   5 6 7 8 9/9 0/0

Printed in the U.S.A.   40

First Scholastic printing, August 1995

FRIENDS FOREVER

THE BABY-SITTERS CLUB

T.M.

THE MOVIE

PROLOGUE

OFFICIAL BABY-SITTERS CLUB NOTEBOOK
SUMMER SESSION

monday

Okay, guys, it's summer vacation but we can't let up. Be there, same times, monday, Wednesday, Friday, 5:30 to 6:00 — SHARP!

No goof-ups, no surprises. A normal summer = happy clients. Don't forget that.

Over and out,
Your president and founder,
Kristy Thomas

Hup two three four!

BSC — Boot Summer Camp!

Heel! Fetch! Roll over!

Ha ha. Very funny. That's what
I get for trying to COMMUNICATE.
No more snide comments — you know
you're supposed to WRITE ABOUT YOUR
JOBS in this book!

Stacey McGill   Tuesday
Arrgh. Marnie Barrett threw
SpaghettiOs at me this afternoon.
I ask you, have you ever tried washing
that stuff out of a brand-new white
shirt?
No way, José. Oh, well, it's time for a
summer shopping trip to NYC, anyway.

Mary Anne Spier   Wednesday

Well, Jackie, Shea, and
Archie Rodowsky were sup-
posed to paint their doghouse
while I sat today.
Instead they painted
their dog.
We washed him three
times, but he's still purple
and yellow.
Sigh. It's a good thing
I'm so patient.

Dawn Schafer   Wednesday
Yyyyes! They said it could

never be done. The odds were overwhelming. Never in four years has anyone attempted this task and survived. Until now.

Let it be known that I, Dawn, got Margie Klinger to eat vegetables today.

The Nobel Peace Prize committee can reach me c/o the BSC.

Claudia Kishi   Thursday

I thot Mrs. Marshel wuld kill me today. I gave Nina some ~~this sizz~~ sissers and showed her how to cut paper dolls.

Wehn I looked up, she was cuting her hare.

I neerly had a hart attact. of coarse I took the siscers away, but the pore thing looked so ~~tha teratl~~ auful. So I did the only thing I could do. I finnishd the harecut.

Know what? Mrs. M didnt kill me. In fact, she paid me xtra and set up another apoinmint!

Mallory Pike   Thursday

Terri and Tammy Barkan have decided they like being identical. They spent the day switching outfits and trying to confuse me. But it didn't work. I was too wise.

My triplet brothers used to do the same thing. Sometimes — just sometimes — it pays to have seven brothers and sisters. You see every trick in the book.

Saturday

Jessica Ramsey

After the Spencer kids saw my ballet recital, they begged me to teach them. So when I sat for them today I brought two pink tutus for the girls and a blue one for Jerry. (Well, he's two. I thought it would be cute.)

When the Spencers came home, they laughed so hard I thought they would barf.

But now Jerry refuses to take his tutu off. The Spencers aren't smiling any more.

CHAPTER **1**

"**D**awn, I hear Alan Gray likes you," said Jessi Ramsey.

Dawn Schafer shivered at the thought. Being liked by Alan Gray was a little like discovering a pimple on your nose: It will always bother you, no matter how hard you try to ignore it. Alan was thirteen, like Dawn, but his maturity level was somewhere between preschool and Neanderthal.

Mallory Pike grinned. "Just likes her? Or . . . *like* likes her?"

"That dweeb?" Dawn said. "Spare me. It doesn't matter anyway, because I don't like him or *like* like him!"

The three girls turned the corner to Bradford Court. Dawn's stepsister, Mary Anne Spier, tagged behind. With a dreamy smile, she gazed at the trees and sniffed the faint scent of honeysuckle.

Summer vacation had just begun for the stu-

1

dents of Stoneybrook Middle School in Stoneybrook, Connecticut. At five-fifteen in the evening, the sun was still strong, but the air had a clear, late-spring coolness.

"Something's wrong here," Mary Anne said with a sigh. "School's out, but I miss it. What's going on?"

"I do, too," Dawn agreed, eager to change the subject from Alan Gray. "It's not that I love it. It's just that — "

" — we won't get to see each other every day," Mary Anne cut in.

"And we end up baby-sitting in different houses," Jessi added.

Mallory nodded. "We might as well be on separate planets."

At 58 Bradford Court, the girls walked up the flagstone pathway and opened the front door. "Hi!" they called out as they walked through the empty living room.

Without waiting for an answer, they bounded up to a small room at the top of the stairs.

Claudia Kishi's bedroom was the official BSC headquarters, mainly because Claudia was the only member with her own phone line. A better name for it, though, might have been the Black Hole of Stoneybrook. Claudia was obsessed with all kinds of art — painting, drawing, sculpture, and jewelry making —

2

and her works-in-progress were all over the place. Next to her bed, an easel was propped against the wall. Tubes of paint, packets of clay, and various paint bottles had been shoved to the side to create some floor space.

Next to Claudia's night table, Kristy Thomas sat on a canvas director's chair, scribbling in the BSC notebook.

"Hi," she grunted, barely looking up.

No one was surprised to see Kristy there alone. She *always* arrived first at the meetings, sometimes even before Claudia.

Kristy was the BSC president. Although she was just five feet tall, she dominated the meetings. But no one minded too much. After all, Kristy had invented the Baby-sitters Club. It had started as a simple idea — a few neighborhood girls who met three times a week to book baby-sitting jobs — but it became much more than that. It became a club of absolute best friends.

As Mary Anne and Dawn sat on Claudia's bed, Jessi and Mallory took their usual places on the carpeted floor. Kristy glanced at the digital clock. It was 5:28, two minutes before meeting time.

Where were Stacey and Claudia? They were hardly ever late. Especially Claudia. In her own house.

Kristy sighed. It was happening, she knew it. The summer slump.

Dawn and Mary Anne were now chatting away, scarfing down a bag of chips. Gray chips.

Kristy nearly gagged. What were those chips made of? Freeze-dried tofu? Baked fungus? Dawn was always eating weird health foods. The eco-baby-sitter, Kristy called her. When Dawn joined the BSC, she had just moved to Stoneybrook from California. Back then, her eating habits and her environmentalism seemed kind of strange. Now the entire BSC was ecologically conscious, but as far as the food? It still made Kristy sick.

It didn't seem to hurt Dawn, though. Her light, freckly skin was without a blemish, and her long blonde hair was without one visible split end.

Kristy stifled a giggle as she watched Mary Anne take a bite. Mary Anne was Kristy's best friend, and they could practically read each other's minds. Right now, Kristy was reading: *These taste like cardboard but I should be polite, for Dawn's sake, and eat some.*

Although Mary Anne and Kristy were about the same size, and both had dark brown hair and eyes, they couldn't have had more different personalities. Mary Anne was as shy and sensitive as Kristy was loud and opinionated.

Kristy couldn't help feeling a twinge of jealousy when she saw how close Mary Anne was to her stepsister. For most of their lives, Mary Anne had lived across the street from Kristy. They had shared their deepest secrets and feelings. Mary Anne's mom had died when she was a baby, and Kristy's father had abandoned the family when Kristy was six.

Not long ago, though, Mr. Spier married Dawn's mom and moved into the Schafers' rambling farmhouse. And Kristy's mom married a millionaire named Watson Brewer, so the Thomas clan (which included Kristy and three brothers) moved clear across town into the Brewer mansion.

Five twenty-nine. Kristy began drumming her fingers on the notebook cover.

Next to her, Jessi Ramsey was carrying on a conversation with Mallory Pike while doing a ballet split. Kristy's bones hurt just to look at Jessi. For an eleven-year-old, she was an amazing dancer. She and Mal were the club's "junior" officers, because they were two years younger than the others, and they were not allowed by their parents to baby-sit at night. Like Mary Anne and Kristy, they were best friends, and different in many ways. Mallory wore glasses, had thick red hair and pale skin, and loved to write and draw. Jessi was African-American, thin and elegant, and

5

wanted more than anything to become a famous ballerina.

Blink. The clock now glowed five-thirty.

"The first Baby-sitters Club meeting of the summer is now called to order!" Kristy blurted out. "Where is everybody?"

The door swung open and Claudia barged in. As always, she looked stunning. Claud was Japanese-American, and Kristy admired her jet-black hair, which today was slicked back with styling mousse. "Sorry, guys," Claudia said. "I was on the phone with my parents."

Kristy raised an eybrow. This did not sound promising. Claudia's last "talk" with her parents was a long lecture about her crazy clothes, her wild hairstyles, her mediocre grades, and her junk-food habit. In other words, the things that made Claudia *Claudia*. As far as Kristy was concerned, the Kishis were way too strict. They always seemed to wish Claudia were a straight-A genius, like her older sister, Janine.

Claudia was now pulling a bag of Hershey's Kisses out of her dresser drawer. She sat on her bed, unwrapping the candies and popping them in her mouth.

Dawn held out her bag of chips. "Claud, do yourself a favor."

Claudia read the label and grimaced. "Soy meal chips? Forget it."

"They're good for sugar addiction."

"So what? Guys, we have a huge crisis on our hands."

Before anyone could say a word, Stacey McGill burst into the room, a shopping bag in each hand.

"I know I'm late," she said breathlessly, "but there was this really big — "

"Sale!" sang Jessi and Mallory together.

Stacey smiled sheepishly. Everyone in the club knew she was a clothes fiend. Her fashion sense was chic and sophisticated, not funky and fun like Claudia's, probably because Stacey was born and raised in New York City.

Like Dawn, Stacey was a daughter of divorced parents. Also like Dawn, Stacey had blonde hair and ate no sweets. But Stacey had a medical reason for her diet. Because of diabetes, her body could not regulate blood sugar — which meant she had to inject herself daily with insulin, eat meals on a strict schedule, and avoid refined sugar.

Sensing Kristy's glaring eyes, Stacey sat in a chair and put her shopping bags behind her.

Claudia didn't even seem to notice Stacey had arrived. Her face was drawn and serious. She swallowed her candy and took a deep breath. "We have a tragedy here," she said.

"I flunked science, and I have to go to summer school."

The words hung in the air like a rain cloud.

"Are your parents going to kill you?" Jessi asked.

"Maybe," Claudia replied.

"Don't worry," Stacey reassured her. "We'll help you."

"You'll pass," Mary Anne agreed. "Promise."

"What if I don't?" said Claudia.

"Don't panic," Kristy insisted. "Panic is for people who are going to fail. And you won't, because we won't let you. Don't worry, it'll be fun."

Claudia stared at her in disbelief. "*Art*'s fun, Kristy. *Dancing*'s fun. *Science* is not fun. It is cruel and unusual punishment."

"You're an artist," Mallory said. "You don't have to be a scientist."

"Tell that to my mom." Claudia sighed. "If I don't get a C-plus, I have to drop out of the club."

Kristy's jaw fell open.

"Whaaaaaat?" cried Mary Anne and Mallory.

"She wouldn't," Jessi insisted.

"She couldn't," Stacey added.

Claudia nodded. "She would. She could."

"But you're a founding member!" Jessi said.

Rrrrringg! The jangling phone cut off the conversation.

"You guys, relax," Kristy said, picking up the receiver. "Baby-sitters Club. . . . Hi, Mrs. Rodowsky!"

Yikes.

Jackie Rodowsky Alert.

Jackie was only seven, but he'd caused enough trouble to last a lifetime. Baby-sitting for the Rodowskys was a little like combat duty.

Mary Anne, Stacey, Dawn, Jessi, and Mallory all waved Kristy off, as if to say *Not me.*

"Six to nine-thirty?" Kristy said into the receiver. "Got it. . . . Yeah, absolutely." She covered the mouthpiece. "Who's free?"

Mary Anne leafed through the BSC record book. As club secretary, she was in charge of all scheduling. "You and me," she said. "But count me out. Last time it took me two hours to get that dog clean."

"Okay, Mrs. Rodowsky, you're all set. I'll be there at six o'clock sharp. Thank you." Kristy hung up. Then she shrugged and said, "I know Jackie Rodowsky's a walking disaster, but I like him. Okay, new business?"

"If I flunk science this summer," Claudia went on, "we can't have our meetings here."

9

"Don't sweat it, Claud," Kristy replied. "I got straight A's in science this year. I'll coach you."

Rrrrringg!

This time Mary Anne picked up the phone. "Baby-sitters Club. . . . A dozen pizzas? I don't think so. Hold on, I'll check."

Dawn grabbed the receiver. *"Toxic waste!"* she shouted and slammed it down.

Kristy, Claudia, Mary Anne, Jessi, and Mallory all gave her a knowing look. Only one person would tie up the BSC phone line with a stupid prank like that. Only one person would be low enough.

"Cokie Mason," Kristy muttered.

Mallory shook her head in disgust. "Loser."

"Oh!" Mary Anne said suddenly. "Stacey, add in the notebook that Logan's brother is allergic to all wheat products and glue."

Stacey picked up a pen, then stopped. *"Glue?"*

Rrrrringg!

"Baby-sitters Club!" Claudia said into the receiver. "Hi, Mrs. Wilder."

As she talked, Dawn whispered to Stacey, "There's wheat in glue."

". . . I'll tell her. 'Bye." Claudia replaced the receiver and called out, "Stace, Mrs. Wilder wants you to know her little nephew will be there tonight. He's from Switzerland."

10

"Great," Stacey said. "I love little kids with accents."

Kristy smiled. Summer slump? What summer slump?

The Baby-sitters Club was off and running.

CHAPTER 2

Stacey heard the violin sonata as she approached the front door of the white house on Elm Street. The music floated into the evening air like a cool breeze.

She smiled. It was hard to believe a seven-year-old could play like that. But violin was only one of Rosie's talents — along with singing, dancing, acting, and art. For a few months, Stacey had been baby-sitting every Wednesday night at the Wilders', and she and Rosie had grown close.

"Hello?" Stacey called out, knocking on the door.

The music stopped. Stacey heard the pounding of feet. The door swung open to reveal a smiling girl holding a long violin bow."Hi, Stacey!" Rosie said.

"Hi, Rosie!"

Stacey leaned down and gave her a hug. Then she presented Rosie with a cardboard box. "There's a special treat in the Kid-Kit for you — extra stickers and puzzles."

Kid-Kits were a Kristy Thomas idea — boxes full of toys, games, and puzzles that BSC members brought along on sitting jobs. Stacey reached in and pulled out a tiny plastic American flag. Waving it daintily in the air, she said, "I also brought a little something for your little cousin. Where is he?"

Out of the corner of her eye, Stacey spotted someone enter the hallway.

Someone male. About seventeen years old.

And drop-dead gorgeous.

Stacey froze.

"I'm Luca, the little cousin," he said with a smile that nearly made Stacey keel over.

And that accent! On kids, it was cute. But on *boys* — real, live, hunkified teenage boys? Devastating. Stacey held onto a chair to brace herself.

"You brought me a gift?" Luca continued.

Stacey's flag suddenly felt pathetic. "Well, it's a little, small . . . American flag . . . thing."

"Cool," Luca said, taking it from her. "Very nationalistic. You're . . . ?"

"Um . . . I'm Stacey, your . . . uh . . ." (Stacey swallowed hard) ". . . uh . . . sitter. I guess."

Rosie gave Luca a curious look. "I thought you were going to the movies."

When Luca answered, he was looking into Stacey's eyes. "I have my whole life to go to the movies."

Stacey hoped Rosie would want to go to bed early that night.

Across town, in front of the Stoneybrook Stables, Kristy pulled firmly at the reins on her horse. It slowed its trot, then stopped. She looked over her shoulder and smiled. Jackie Rodowsky was still on his horse, yanking the reins a little too hard, but managing well nonetheless. Behind him, Mary Anne and her boyfriend, Logan Bruno, brought their horses to a stop. It had been a good ride.

As Kristy, Mary Anne, and Logan praised Jackie for his progress, Cokie Mason emerged from the stable. Her friends, Grace Blume and Bebe Hanson, followed close behind. They tugged on their helmets and fussed with their brand-new, top-of-the-line riding gear.

"Your helmet's on backward," Cokie said to Grace.

"It hurts my ears the other way," Grace complained.

Cokie grabbed Grace's helmet and turned it around. Her friends were cool. They stayed in line. They did as they were told. But boy, were they dense.

As Grace winced with pain, Cokie turned to watch the girls in the Baby-sitters Club. "Uch," she said. "Look at Kristy and her band of goody two-shoes. What do they think they are, a family?"

But Cokie's eyes were focused on Mary Anne, not Kristy. Mary Anne and Logan were grinning at each other, all lovey-dovey. *What did he see in her?* Cokie couldn't figure it out. He was cute, a great athlete, and not stuck on himself. His wavy blondish-brown hair, his dimples, his Southern accent — perfect. A guy like that didn't deserve to go out with a wimp. He needed someone cool, someone fun.

Someone like, oh, say, Cokie Mason.

Now the two lovebirds were brushing their horses. "Did you bring the carrots?" Cokie could hear Logan ask.

"Yeah, they're in my back pocket," Mary Anne replied.

Her horse nuzzled his head around Mary Anne and took the carrot right out of her pocket. Logan burst out laughing.

"I know you taught him to do that," Mary Anne said.

"I did not," Logan insisted.

"Oh, right, they were born knowing how to do that."

Logan shrugged. "A horse would do anything for a carrot."

How . . . cute. How too, too cute. Cokie wanted to throw up.

From behind her, Grace whispered, "What if she doesn't leave him alone?"

"Mary Anne and Logan never let each other out of their sight," Bebe said.

Cokie grinned. "What are they afraid of? *Moi?*"

Now Mary Anne was walking toward the tack room to put away the horses' brushes and hoof pick. Logan was with Kristy, helping Jackie dismount.

This was it. The perfect time for Cokie's plan.

Cokie and her friends approached Kristy.

"Logan, I'm *so* glad you're here!" Cokie said, giving him her deepest, most sincere smile. "I wanted to call you."

Kristy glared at her. "Get lost, Cokie."

"Hello, *Kristin*." Cokie's eyes dropped toward Jackie. "Oh, you have a date. And I see his age is the same as your IQ."

"Who let you out of the bat cave, *Marguerite*?" Kristy shot back.

"She hates to be called that," Bebe muttered to Grace.

"That's your real name?" Grace asked.

"No," Cokie replied. "It's the mumbling of an idiot."

16

Cokie took Logan's arm and gave a quick nod to her friends.

Bebe and Grace scurried inside the tack room. There, they found Mary Anne hanging her helmet on the wall.

Mary Anne eyed them warily. "Hi."

"Hi," Grace and Bebe repeated.

"Excuse me," Mary Anne said. As she walked past them toward the door, Grace gave Bebe a look of panic.

"Did you get your hair cut?" Bebe blurted out.

Mary Anne stopped. "No."

"It must look like that from your helmet," Bebe remarked.

Ignoring the comment, Mary Anne continued walking toward the door.

"*Wait!*" Grace shouted.

Mary Anne turned again. What was with these girls? Had they upped the dosage of their daily weird pills?

"Uh, what classes are you going to take next year?" Grace asked.

Bebe rolled her eyes. Mary Anne stared blankly.

"Can I try on your riding pants?" Grace asked.

That did it. Enough was enough. Mary Anne walked out of the tack room.

Cokie was deep in conversation with Logan. "Fifth row, center?" Mary Anne heard Logan say. "How did you get them?"

Cokie's eyes darted toward Mary Anne, then back to Logan. "I knew you'd say yes!" she said loudly. "Just think: you, me, and Smashing Pumpkins!"

With that, she spun away. "But Cokie — I — " Logan stammered.

Mary Anne hated confrontation. She usually avoided the slightest hint of an argument. But this was going too far. "Cokie!" she called out.

Cokie turned and glared at her. *"What?"*

The words caught in Mary Anne's throat. Her lips began to quiver, and tears welled up in her eyes. Cokie's mocking, icy-cold expression blurred.

"Don't waste my time," Cokie snapped. "Logan, call me tomorrow."

As Cokie and her friends left, Logan began turning red.

"Logan, I don't believe you," Mary Anne said, her voice quivering.

Before Logan could defend himself, Kristy and Jackie took Mary Anne by the arm and led her away.

CHAPTER 3

At the Wilders' house, Luca and Stacey sat on the living room couch. In the quiet of the night-darkened house, Luca played a few bars of mournful music on his harmonica.

Stacey could have stayed there forever. But Mr. and Mrs. Wilder soon came home and Rosie came back downstairs.

Stacey didn't want to say good-bye to Luca. Instead she said, "Thanks for helping me baby-sit." Reaching into her pocket, she pulled out her earnings and handed part of the money to Luca. "Here, it's half of what I made tonight."

Luca shook his head. "No, keep the money."

Stacey put it back into her pocket. With each step closer to the door, she felt grimmer. In a few moments she would leave the Wilders, and a whole week would trudge by. It didn't seem fair.

19

"So," Stacey said, "I guess . . . uh, well, I baby-sit for Rosie every Wednesday — "

"From seven-thirty to nine-thirty," Rosie chimed in.

Luca's face was somehow twice as handsome when he smiled. "What about every other night of your life?" he asked. "Do you like the cinema?"

Stacey's heart felt like a jackhammer. Her throat was dry.

"*Mary Poppins* is her favorite," Rosie said. "We've seen the video a hundred thousand times."

Oh, groan. *Mary Poppins?* "Uh, I *loved* the special effects," Stacey quickly added.

"Go out with me Saturday," Luca said. "Show me around Stoneybrook."

"Oh, there's not much to see," Stacey replied. "It's not like New York City. That's where I grew up. Have you ever been there?"

Luca shook his head. "Not yet."

"It's the best," Stacey said.

"You mean, like you," Luca added.

Gulp.

Stacey turned to face Luca. His smile was like Christmas.

Then, slowly, he leaned closer.

Stacey's eyes widened. It couldn't be happening. It was too wonderful, too perfect . . .

"Are you going to kiss her?" Rosie asked hopefully.

Luca burst out laughing.

Thank you, Rosie.

Stacey wanted to strangle her.

"Whatever gave you that idea, Rosalind?" Luca said. Then, turning to Stacey, he added, "I'll ring you."

Stacey headed out the door and down the Wilders' walkway.

She could barely put one foot in front of the other.

CHAPTER 4

Kristy could hardly hear Mary Anne on the other end of the portable phone. As she stood in the family room door, her little brother David Michael and adopted sister Emily Michelle ran by, screaming at the top of their lungs.

Kristy was used to the noise. The size of the Brewer mansion seemed to make every sound twice as loud.

It was a Wednesday, one week since Cokie had pulled her stunt at the stables, and still Mary Anne hadn't been able to talk to Logan.

"Mary Anne, is he going to the concert with her or not?" Kristy shouted into the phone.

Watson, Kristy's stepfather, bounded through the room after the two kids.

Kristy listened to Mary Anne as well as she could, then said, "Well, ask him! . . . What do you mean you can't? You have to!"

Charlie and Sam, Kristy's older brothers,

huffed through the hallway outside the door. They were about to leave for an overnight camping trip a half hour away, but they were dragging enough packs and duffles to outfit an expedition to the Alps. Behind them was Kristy's mom.

As Charlie passed Kristy, he gave her ponytail a gentle tug. "Mom, I can't find my keys to the Junk Bucket!" he called over his shoulder.

"Anyway, if he does go," Kristy said to Mary Anne, "we'll shave his head!"

Her ear still glued to the phone, Kristy followed her brothers and her mom out to the front lawn. Charlie and Sam were loading their stuff into a rusty, dented sedan that looked as if it had escaped from a junkyard.

"You are not driving that to the train station," Mrs. Brewer insisted. "It doesn't even have a horn."

"I'm bringing my own," said Charlie. He held up a black electronic box and pressed a button on top. Out blared the theme song from *My Three Sons*.

"I have to go," Kristy said into the phone. "My brothers are leaving. I'll call you later."

She pressed the off button.

"Charlie, you have to take my car," Mrs. Brewer was saying to Charlie and Sam. "Watson and I will get it later."

"Really?"

"Oh, don't act so surprised." Mrs. Brewer shook her head. "You left me all the Park Rangers' numbers, right?"

"Yes," Sam replied. "All eight of them."

Mrs. Brewer handed Charlie the keys. As the boys kissed their mom good-bye, Watson walked out the front door and waved.

" 'Bye, Watson!" Charlie shouted, climbing into the front seat. " 'Bye, Kristy! 'Bye, noisy house!"

" 'Bye!" Kristy shouted back.

"Don't clean my room while I'm gone!" Charlie added, as he backed the car out of the driveway.

They all watched the car disappear down McLelland Road, then walked toward the front door.

"Have you seen Karen and Andrew?" Watson asked.

Seven-year-old Karen and four-year-old Andrew were Watson's children from his first marriage. Right now they were living with Watson; every other month they lived with their mom.

"Weren't they with David Michael and Emily Michelle?" Mrs. Brewer asked. She shook her head and sighed. "This house is too big."

Click. A lightbulb went off in Kristy's head.

If Claudia flunked science, the BSC would need a new headquarters, and a new phone. The Brewer mansion had only one measly phone line for the whole, huge, rambling house.

"Mom, can I have my own phone?" Kristy asked.

"No," Mrs. Brewer replied.

"But I need it for business."

"Not until you're sixteen."

"Kristy," Watson asked, "have you seen Karen and Andrew?"

His words were lost on Kristy. "But Mom, that doesn't make any sense!"

"It doesn't have to," Mrs. Brewer retorted.

They walked inside, following Watson as he peered into all the first-floor rooms. "I looked in the garage," he said, "and I looked upstairs."

"You can't just say no," Kristy insisted, ignoring Watson. "A good parent would give her child a logical reason."

"Fine," Mrs. Brewer replied. "I don't want you to become spoiled."

"I'm already spoiled!"

Watson stormed into and out of his office, his forehead creased with frustration.

"Honey, they're here somewhere," Mrs. Brewer said.

"Where?" Watson asked. "I looked in the laundry room, all the bathrooms, under the beds, and in the garage."

"I know!" Kristy said brightly. "They're with Colonel Mustard in the library with the wrench."

Kristy's mom glowered at her. Watson jogged toward the back of the house.

With a shrug, Kristy joined the search. She began by pulling open the door to the basement.

At the bottom of the stairs, Karen looked up. She was wearing a dish towel on her head. Andrew stood beside her with a plunger strapped to his leg and a watch hanging loosely around his wrist.

"I'm pirate Esmerelda," Karen announced. "And this is my slave."

Kristy laughed. She realized the plunger was supposed to be a peg leg.

Watson appeared at the door. "And that's my grandfather's antique watch. Come here, mateys!"

He scooped up his giggling pirates and carried them away.

"What would you guys do without me?" Kristy said.

CHAPTER 5

"Mmmmm," said Claudia.

Nothing could beat the smell of fresh-baked chocolate-chip cookies, Claudia thought. As she pulled them out of the oven, Dawn and Kristy prepared the rest of the afternoon's snacks — popcorn and glasses of milk.

The kitchen clock read 5:27. Almost time for the Friday BSC meeting. Stacey was sitting at the table, carefully testing her blood sugar.

"Do you think I should have told Luca about my diabetes?" Stacey asked.

"It's not like the flu or something," Kristy replied. "He can't catch it."

"If he's any kind of guy, he won't care," Dawn insisted.

"I don't want him to know," Stacey said. "He'll think I'm pathetic."

"Everybody else knows, and they don't think you're pathetic," Kristy said. "A little psycho, maybe."

Claudia picked up a pot of melted butter and began to pour butter into the popcorn, but Dawn pushed her arm away.

"He also doesn't know I'm thirteen," Stacey added. "He's seventeen."

"He's a poet," Claudia said.

"He drives," Stacey countered.

Claudia shrugged. "He's a musical genius."

"He's been to Europe," Stacey said.

"He's *from* Europe," Kristy reminded her.

As everyone left the kitchen, Claudia put some popcorn for herself in a small bowl, poured the butter on it, and followed the girls upstairs.

The meeting began at five-thirty sharp, with a treasurer's report from Stacey.

"After dues we'll have fifty-eight dollars," she said. "But after the phone bill and Kid-Kit supplies, we have eleven dollars and forty-seven cents."

"Okay. New business," Kristy announced. "I have a brilliant idea."

She pulled a flier from her jeans pocket and handed it to Mary Anne.

Mary Anne read it aloud. "'Stoneybrook Summer Camp for Seniors'?"

"No, a day camp for our clients," Kristy replied. "It gives us a new service to offer, it'll be a total gold mine, and most important, it's a way for us to stay together all summer." She grinned triumphantly. "Is this not the most brilliant idea yet?"

The girls stared at her blankly. "She's in the zone," Dawn remarked.

"She's out of control," Claudia said.

"Last time she was like this, she wanted us to open a dude ranch," Stacey added.

"The kids will love it!" Kristy insisted. "And it'll be so easy. We'll go from ten to four, Monday through Friday. We'll start after the Fourth of July, which'll give us enough time to get ready, and we'll go through Labor Day. We'll figure out what to charge later." She pulled out more folded sheets from her pocket. "I've taken the liberty of putting together a schedule and start-up budget for you guys to check out."

She passed the papers around. As the other girls read them, they began nodding solemnly. Kristy's plan actually made sense. On paper, at least.

"Kristy," Jessi remarked, "*this* brilliant idea might really be brilliant."

Rule Number One of the Kristy Thomas Theory of Brilliant Ideas: Location is everything.

The first choice for the campground was

Mary Anne and Dawn's yard. The yard beside the farmhouse was big, and the barn would be perfect for equipment storage.

On Saturday, while Mary Anne and Dawn asked their parents' permission, the other members of the BSC gathered outside.

Dawn emerged from the house with a smile. "They said we could use the yard!"

Behind her, Mary Anne held up a sheaf of papers. "But here are a few rules. The first, in bold print and underlined: 'The house is off-limits to all children.' "

"At all times," Dawn added.

"Okay, let's start marking off the yard," Kristy said. "We'll need a sports area, dance area . . ."

"A first-aid tent by the barn," Mary Anne suggested.

"We can put the Porta Potties over there." Kristy pointed toward the picket fence that separated the house from the one next door.

"Perfect," Stacey said. "Then we can line the garbage cans right up against the fence."

"Oh, you guys, I forgot," Mary Anne said. "My dad wants these contracts signed."

As the girls gathered around, a pair of eyes watched them through the fence.

Mrs. Emily Haberman lived next door to the Schafer/Spiers. She hadn't minded the family at all, until now.

Her wildflower garden, the pride of her life, lay just inside the fence. Just beyond where the camp garbage cans and lunch area were going to be set up.

Mrs. Haberman did not like that idea. Not one bit.

CHAPTER 6

Rule Number Two of the Kristy Thomas Theory of Brilliant Ideas: No idea is great without great advertising.

On Sunday, Claudia designed fliers. (Kristy helped with the spelling.) The next day, Operation Summer Camp began.

Kristy handed out fliers at a softball practice. Claudia posted some on the summer school bulletin board. Jessi and Mallory distributed some at the stables. Dawn stapled three to the Stoneybrook community bulletin board on Main Street. Claudia and Stacey made an announcement over the radio station.

Thursday they all treated themselves to dinner at Burger Town. On the way in, Dawn and Mary Anne stapled a flier to a bulletin board just inside the front door.

The girls walked to their favorite booth in the back, and ordered enormous custom-made burgers — except for Dawn, who chose a salad with a side of roasted sunflower seeds.

Across the crowded floor, they could not see Cokie, Bebe, and Grace entering on Rollerblades.

Cokie ripped off the flier and read it. She thought for a few moments, and then her face lit up.

Turning on her skates, Cokie shooed her friends back out the door. As they rolled onto the street, she whispered a plan to them.

In the restaurant, the BSC members tore into their food. Stacey somehow managed to finish off a burger while furiously adding up numbers on a sheet of paper.

"Isn't it great how every time we come in here, the food tastes exactly the same?" Kristy said. "Something you can count on."

Jessi caught a glimpse of Dawn swallowing a forkful of sprouts. "Hey, Dawn, have you watered yourself lately?"

"What?" Dawn asked blankly.

As the table erupted in giggles, Claudia said, "Kristy, you have a birthday coming up. What should we do?"

"Oh, I don't care," Kristy replied. "As long as it's the best day of my life. But no pressure."

Stacey slapped her pencil down. "You are not going to believe this. At two hundred fifty dollars per camper, if thirty campers sign up, even after expenses, we are left with a profit of four thousand seven hundred fifty dollars!"

"We're rich!" Claudia exclaimed.

"We can almost buy a car," Jessi said.

"Yeah, and in five years we can drive it," Mallory added.

"If we make enough, maybe we can get an office, open our doors to the world!" Kristy went on. "Oh, and Stace, we need to add box drinks to our list."

"Our own office," Stacey said. "That's a great idea."

"We could get a fax machine," Mallory suggested.

"That would sure let me off the hook if I flunk," Claudia remarked.

In unison, Stacey and Kristy said, "You're not going to flunk!"

"I say we start looking," Dawn urged.

"How many people have we actually signed up?" Mary Anne asked.

"At last count — " Stacey glanced at her notes. "Twelve."

Kristy, Claudia, Dawn, Mallory, and Jessi slumped in their seats. "We passed out a million fliers!" Dawn said.

"Everyone will sign up at the last minute," Kristy assured her.

"They'd better," Mary Anne remarked. "We start Monday."

"How's your little camp going?" asked a familiar, grating voice.

The girls looked up to see Cokie approaching with her two goons in tow.

"Great," Kristy said. "Couldn't be better."

"Really?" Cokie held out a fistful of crumpled-up papers. "Well, I just happened to find a few of these just kind of . . . flying around Main Street."

She opened her fist, and the papers fell onto the table — all BSC Summer Camp fliers.

Kristy, Stacey, Dawn, Claudia, Mary Anne, Jessi, and Mallory stared in shocked silence.

Turning to leave, Cokie said, "Oh, Mary Anne, I bought the most *outrageous* outfit for the concert."

With that, she led her friends to a nearby booth and sat down.

"I'm not going to cry," Mary Anne said under her breath.

Kristy's mind was racing. She sprang up from the table. "Don't anybody go anywhere."

She did not wait to answer any bewildered questions. Instead she walked calmly to Cokie's booth. "Listen, you guys," she said, "we've been fighting each other since the third grade. Now that we're getting a little older, don't you think it's time to stop?"

Grace and Bebe looked at Cokie. For once, Cokie was at a loss for words.

"We're having our annual BSC party at Miller's Park," Kristy went on. "Tomorrow, eight o'clock. If you can come, it'd be great. Eight o'clock, sharp."

She gave them the biggest smile she could manage. Then she strolled back to her booth.

Back to six gaping, totally baffled friends.

"What party?" Jessi asked.

Kristy shushed her. The explanation would come later. After Cokie was out of earshot.

And boy, was it a good one.

That night, Claudia could think of nothing but camp. She stared blankly at her science textbook. Her first quiz was the next day, and she might as well have been looking at a book written in Norwegian.

She closed it and took her calendar from the wall. Over July 5 she wrote *First day of camp*. Then she began doodling.

From the bottom of the stairs, her mother called, "Claudia, are you studying?"

Claudia quickly opened the book again.

"Uh-huh," she said, and continued her drawing.

* * *

The next evening, Cokie, Bebe, and Grace strolled into Miller's Park. Their clothes, their hair, their makeup — everything was perfect. Just cool enough to make the BSC members look about as exciting as oatmeal.

They glanced around. The grassy field was totally empty. Cokie checked her watch. Seven fifty-nine. Weird. Those girls were never late.

"Now what?" Bebe asked.

Beep! Cokie's watch signaled eight o'clock.

Shhhhhhhiiiiish! All around them, the sprinkler heads began turning on.

Water blasted the girls from all sides. Cokie shrieked. They were instantly soaked.

This was low. Low and dirty.

This meant war.

CHAPTER 7

"Kids under seven this way!" Mallory shouted.

"Kids over seven this way!" Jessi called.

Monday, July fifth, had arrived. It was the first day of camp, and the Baby-sitters Club was prepared. As cars pulled up to the curb, kids swarmed onto the BSC Summer Camp grounds.

Logan Bruno and Alan Gray strolled down the sidewalk and stopped to watch. Logan tried to catch Mary Anne's glance, but she was busy.

Alan was not nearly as shy. With a goofball grin, he bounded over to Mallory. "What about guys over thirteen?" he asked.

"Better see the boss," Mallory replied.

No one could mistake who that was. Near the picket fence, Kristy sat behind a registration table. The word *Boss* was printed across her green cap.

She stood up, holding a megaphone to her mouth.

"Welcome to the official opening of the first day of the Baby-sitters Club Summer Day Camp!" her voice blared.

"YEEEEAAAAAAAA!" shouted the campers.

Next door, Mrs. Haberman was jolted from an outdoor nap. Her book, which had been lying open on her chest, went flying into her bowl of popcorn.

As it spilled onto her lap, Mrs. Haberman shot a furious glance toward the chaos next door.

"On behalf of every one of our baby-sitters, I have a souvenir for you," Kristy announced, holding up potholders of different colors. The BSC phone number was printed on each one. "It also serves an important purpose. It connects you with your counselor. Don't hesitate to show it to your friends and family."

The campers rushed to the table. Stacey and Claudia gave the kids name tags, and Dawn handed out the color-coded potholders.

"Look, Kristy!" Jackie Rodowsky held up his potholder. "Green!"

Kristy tapped the green potholder pinned to her shirt and gave him a thumbs-up.

Nearby, four-year-old Nina Marshall asked Dawn, "Can I have one for Jimmytony?"

"How old is he?" Dawn asked.

Nina turned to the empty space beside her. "Jimmytony, she wants to know how old you are." She fell silent for a moment, as if listening, then turned back to Dawn. "He's the same age as me."

"Well then, he gets a red one, too," Dawn said.

As Nina "pinned" a potholder on her imaginary friend, Margie Klinger stalked toward Mallory with a scowl.

"Margie, how old are you?" Mallory asked.

"Who wants to know?" Margie retorted.

Mallory gave her a blue potholder and pushed her toward Jessi. "She's in your group."

Stacey and Kristy smiled as eight-year-old Buddy Barrett led his little sister, Suzi, by the hand toward the table. Suzi was chewing on the ends of her hair and looking around in confusion.

"Uh, my mom was wondering," Buddy said, "well, there's two of us, and my mom and dad are divorced now, so my mom was wondering if we could both get in for the price of one."

"I've been to the moon," Suzi added earnestly, as if that would help.

Stacey looked at Kristy. Kristy shrugged and stamped *paid* in the official ledger book over both kids' names.

As they scampered away, Mallory was putting a name tag on Jamie Newton. Jamie immediately reached into his pocket and pulled out a Band-Aid. He placed it over his name and beamed triumphantly.

Stacey's face fell as she saw Alan Gray approach. "Oh, no," she murmured. "The neb."

"Hide me," Dawn pleaded.

"You guys need some help?" Alan asked.

"We may be desperate," Kristy replied, "but we're not insane."

"You sure?" Alan pressed on. "My dad has a woodworking shop."

Dawn rolled her eyes. "Is his name Geppetto?"

"Hi, Stacey!"

At the sound of Luca's voice, Stacey nearly jumped out of her seat. She looked up to see Luca and Rosie. "I'll be right back," she whispered to Kristy.

"Hi, Luca," she said with a smile, stepping around the table.

As the two of them walked off, Dawn, Claudia, and Kristy watched Luca carefully.

"You can breathe now," Alan said.

"He's a force of nature." Dawn sighed.

"I love his earring," Claudia remarked.

"What's he got that I don't have?" Alan asked.

Dawn and Claudia gave him a withering glance. "Everything."

Not far away, hidden by the crowd, eight-year-old Nicky Pike reached into a box of doughnuts. His friends, Daniel, Emmy, and Jonas, were rigging up a slingshot out of sticks and broken balloons.

Together, they shot a jelly doughnut high into the air. It flew over the picket fence and into the next yard.

Mrs. Haberman saw it and ducked. The doughnut sailed over her head and wedged itself in one of her birdfeeders.

Her face turned a deep, angry shade of red.

After registration, Mary Anne began setting up a puppet show in the drama area. When Logan offered to help her, she could barely speak. How dare he show up on such a busy day, especially after what had happened at the stables?

"Look, Mary Anne, I didn't say yes to Cokie," Logan pleaded.

Mary Anne unclenched her teeth. "But you didn't say no."

"I wasn't going to go with her," Logan insisted. "Really."

Behind a hedge near the sidewalk, Cokie and her two friends watched the conversation silently. "Ladies," Cokie whispered, "we could do some major damage here."

The camp day was only an hour old when Jonas dropped out of a three legged race to tell Kristy, "I have to go to the bathroom."

"Me, too!" said Jackie, running up beside him.

Bathroom!

Kristy ran to the arts and crafts area and pulled Claudia aside. "Where are the Porta Potties?"

"I don't know," Claudia answered. "The guy said they were coming at eight o'clock this morning."

"I have to go now!" Jonas shrieked.

Matt Braddock, a profoundly deaf camper, ran up. He signed that he had to go, too.

"Mary Anne," Kristy said, "we have to use your house."

"No way," Mary Anne replied. "My dad will kill us."

But the girls had no choice. Reluctantly, Mary Anne led the line of jiggling, complaining campers to the downstairs bathroom. Suzi was one of the first to go inside.

The line grew longer. Three minutes passed,

then five . . . kids were beginning to dance in agony.

Mary Anne knocked on the door and whispered, "Uh, Suzi, what are you doing?"

"Shaving," Suzi replied.

Mary Anne pushed open the door. Suzi's face was covered with shaving cream. With a comb, she was happily scraping it off.

At that moment, summer camp suddenly did not seem as if it were such a brilliant idea at all.

By the time parents began collecting their children, Kristy was exhausted. The day had gone quickly, but it had been even more work than she'd expected. Her shoulders ached as she lugged equipment back into the barn.

She passed Alan and Logan, who were performing magic tricks for the remaining campers. With a flourish, Alan pulled an egg out of Jamie's ear. It fell to the ground with a dull splat.

The kids screamed with delight.

Alan smiled at Kristy. "Are you sure you guys don't need any free help? This is my last offer."

"Sounds like your first offer," Kristy remarked. Around her, the other BSC members were looking just as tired as she felt. But the word *help* had a magic effect. No one was going to argue with Alan now.

Kristy sighed. "When can you start?"

"Yesterday!" Alan replied.

"It's a deal."

Dawn looked astonished. "Kristy!"

"He'll be a trainee," Kristy assured her. "Look, I'm camp director."

"He's a dweeb!" Dawn shot back.

"He's a free dweeb," Kristy reminded her.

"Yeah!" Alan shouted defiantly. "I'm a free dweeb."

Suddenly water squirted from a trick flower Alan had pinned to his shirt. He cracked up.

Kristy gritted her teeth. He had better be worth it.

Mary Anne and Kristy biked to the Brewer house together after camp.

"Logan told me he wouldn't have gone," Mary Anne said as they turned up McLelland Road.

"But what if he did?" Kristy asked. "What would you have done?"

Mary Anne shrugged. "Nothing."

"You *couldn't* do nothing."

"If he wants to do something, I can't stop him."

"Yes, you can. You can tell somebody when

you're ticked off. I mean, we can't let men get away with everything."

The girls pulled up in front of Kristy's house and got off their bikes.

"Kristy!"

The voice made Kristy's body clench. It was a man's voice, at once strange and deeply familiar.

She swung around. A van she'd never seen before was parked at the curb. Its driver was leaning against it and smiling.

As he walked toward her, Kristy realized she was looking into the face of her father.

CHAPTER 8

The man's eyes were moist. "Kristy, it's me."

"Dad?" Kristy's voice was a dry squeak. Could it be? The face was different. Older, thinner. But the smile, the tilt of the head, the sad eyes, could be no one else's.

"You shaved your beard," was all Kristy could think to say.

"Yeah, awhile ago." Kristy's dad nodded awkwardly, then glanced at Mary Anne. "And you're Kristy's friend . . ."

"Mary Anne," said Mary Anne softly. "Uh, I guess I'd better go. It was nice, uh, seeing you again, Mr. Thomas."

"Patrick," he replied.

"Call me later," Mary Anne whispered to Kristy. Quickly she climbed back on her bike and pedaled away.

In silence, Kristy and her dad watched Mary Anne disappear down the street.

"Sorry," Patrick finally said, "I didn't mean to surprise you like this."

"What are you doing here?" Kristy asked.

"Didn't you get my postcard? I said I'd be coming."

"You always say you'll be coming."

Kristy looked at the ground. She tried to fight the anger that was bubbling up inside her.

"So, how are you doing?" Patrick asked. "You look great. What, it's been . . . you used to be — "

"Six," Kristy said flatly.

Patrick took a deep breath. "How are Sam and Charlie?"

"They're backpacking," Kristy answered.

"Good, they're still doing that. How's the baby?"

"Baby? David Michael's seven."

"I know," Patrick said with a solemn nod. "Uh, you hungry? Want to go for a pizza?"

Kristy looked her dad square in the eye. "Why are you here?"

"I know this is weird, just showing up," Patrick replied, "but I couldn't think of another way to do it."

"Do what?"

"I'm moving back," Patrick replied. "I have a shot at a sports column for the *News*."

Kristy didn't know how to take that. Part of her wanted to jump with joy, but another part wished he'd never shown up.

When Patrick spoke again, his voice was gentle and apologetic. "I wanted the job to be a sure thing before I saw you. But seeing you just now, I couldn't resist my favorite girl."

Kristy steeled herself against crying. She couldn't let him win her back so easily. "What happened in L.A.?" she asked.

Her dad shrugged. "Didn't work out. You know how it goes."

"The marriage or the job?"

"Both."

"Did you see Mom?"

"Not yet."

"She's probably home."

"I don't want her to know I'm here yet," Patrick said. "Not until I hear about the job. Think you can keep it between us for a couple of days?"

Kristy nodded. "I guess."

With a smile, Patrick said, "I like your hair long like that. You look real cool." He opened the van's front door and climbed in. "If you need me, I'm at the Strathmore Inn. Don't forget, I owe you a pizza. Still like anchovies best?"

With a grin that tore at Kristy's heart, he

pulled away from the curb and drove off. Kristy stood there, frozen for a moment, then turned back toward her house.

"Kristy, I don't brake for animals!"

Cokie Mason zoomed by on Rollerblades, missing Kristy by inches. Kristy fell back, losing her balance.

"Oh, and tell your friends," Cokie shouted over her shoulder, "I don't get mad, I get even!"

Throwing her head back with laughter, Cokie picked up speed.

For once, Kristy didn't have a comeback line. She was numb.

Somehow, Cokie didn't seem very important just then.

The next day, shortly before the start of camp, a truck pulled up to the Schafer/Spier house with the two portable toilets that Kristy had rented. As workers set them up, Dawn and Logan tacked *Boys* and *Girls* signs over the doors.

Neither Kristy nor Mary Anne helped out. Near the barn, they were involved in an intense, private conversation.

Dawn glanced at them curiously and turned to Logan. He smiled and shrugged. These days, he didn't know what was on Mary Anne's mind.

50

Dawn walked over to her group and began an ecology workshop, planting seeds into soil packed in egg cartons.

"Hey, Dawn!" Alan called out, walking toward her backward on his hands.

Crunch. His palm landed on one of the egg cartons. It flipped over, sending seeds and dirt flying.

Dawn groaned. "Alan, why do you act like such a bonehead?"

Alan tumbled to his feet and stood up. "No good reason," he said sheepishly.

In the farthest portion of the yard, Kristy was coaching a softball game. She watched as Matt Braddock pitched to Jackie Rodowsky, who already had nine consecutive strikes.

When Jackie saw that the outfielders were sitting down, he took a ferocious swing.

He missed the ball completely. The bat whipped around and whacked his toe. "Yeeeeeeeeooooow!" he screamed.

"Good cut, Jackie, but we have a little work to do," Kristy said. "How's the toe?"

Jackie smiled. "What toe?"

In the first-aid tent, Mallory was putting a Band-Aid on Jamie's finger, which already sported three Band-Aids.

Logan passed by, holding Margie Klinger by the arm. "Mallory, Margie is on a time-out for sticking gum in Charlotte's hair," he reported as he set her down on a cot. "How old are you, Margie?"

"Four and a half," she grumbled.

"You're on a four-and-a-half-minute time-out," Logan commanded.

"No, I'm two!" Margie quickly said.

Near the end of the day, Kristy began to panic. In a few minutes, she would meet her dad at the park. What would he be like? Would he approve of her? Would he blame her for making him leave the family?

She had talked Mary Anne into going with her, for moral support. Still, her heart was pounding like crazy.

Kristy ran to the art area, where Mary Anne and Claudia were leading a finger-painting session.

"Mary Anne," Kristy called out, "we have to go."

"We do?" Mary Anne looked at her, baffled. Then she remembered. "Oh, yeah, we do."

"Claudia, can you oversee cleanup and take care of those extra supplies for me?" Kristy said. "Thanks, you're the best."

"But I have to — " Claudia protested.

Kristy and Mary Anne were off and running.

"Study," Claudia continued weakly. "I have to study."

52

CHAPTER 9

F.

Fail.

Flunk.

Forget about the BSC.

It was the ugliest letter of the alphabet, Claudia was convinced. And she could not stop thinking about it.

After camp, she had invited Dawn to take a walk with her. Together the girls ambled down Burnt Hill Road. As they talked, they passed an old, abandoned lot next to Mrs. Haberman's house.

"I get home, I open the book, and I just stare," Claudia said. "Nothing goes in."

Dawn nodded sympathetically.

Claudia stopped short. "What a cool place. What is it?"

She had her eyes on the lot. In the middle of it, overgrown with weeds, was an old brick building.

"It's a greenhouse," Dawn replied. "Or it used to be."

"It's major," Claudia said. "I have to sit down."

"What's wrong?"

"I think I'm having my first brilliant idea."

Half a block from Miller's Park, Mary Anne stopped pedaling. "Kristy, I don't know. I don't really belong there."

"Please, Mary Anne, come with me," Kristy pleaded. "I don't want to go there alone."

Mary Anne took a deep breath and continued.

As the girls biked into the park, the sun was setting. Patrick's van was parked in a secluded area. Next to it, he'd set up a small folding table with three chairs.

"Hi!" Patrick called out from the van's kitchenette. "Kristy, you're going to love what I'm cooking. I hope Mary Anne does, too."

"That's okay," Mary Anne said. "I don't have to eat. I can even leave."

Kristy gave her a sharp look. "No. She'll eat anything."

The girls leaned their bikes against a tree, and Patrick set out two plates, covered with paper towels. As the girls sat down, he yanked off the towels. "Da da da-da!"

Each plate held a batch of tiny, steaming, moist-looking pancakes.

"Mouse pancakes!" Kristy said, fighting back a smile. "Wow, Dad — I mean, Patrick."

Mary Anne looked horrified. "What's in them?"

"Pancake mix," Patrick replied. "When Kristy was little, the only way I could get her to eat was to make these tiny pancakes. So we did, every Sunday morning. Right, partner?"

The smile was so warm and loving. Kristy wanted badly to let it in. But she couldn't. After what he'd done, it had taken years for the hurt to fade. She would not let herself be torn apart again.

"When are you going to call Mom?" she asked.

"Soon," Patrick replied. "I've been pretty busy."

"A phone call doesn't take that much time," Kristy said.

Mary Anne stood up. "I'm going to go to the bathroom."

As she headed off toward the outdoor restrooms, Patrick sat at the table. When he spoke, his voice was gentle and sincere. "Kristy, your mom thinks I'm a loser. So when I walk in that mansion you live in now, I need to have a job and a home — be a little set up, you know? Chris Almond at the paper told me it'd be a few more days. A week, tops. Can you give me that?"

"I guess so," Kristy replied.

"Hey, I have something for you." Patrick stood up, pulled a box from inside the camper, and handed it to Kristy.

She opened it and took out a light, summery dress.

Kristy could hardly remember the last time she had worn a dress. Her mom had practically had to bribe her to put it on.

"Thanks," she said.

Patrick looked concerned. "What? If you don't like it, I can return it."

"No, I like it. It's nice, for a dress," She smiled as sweetly as she could, folded it back into the box, and dug into her mouse pancakes.

As darkness fell, Kristy and Mary Anne thanked Patrick and biked to Kristy's house. Mary Anne had gotten permission to sleep over.

When they arrived, they headed straight for Kristy's room. For the first time in years, Kristy reached into the back of her closet and pulled out a small, taped-shut shoebox. Inside were photos of her and her dad — photos she had removed from family albums long ago.

They whiled away time until the house grew

quiet. Then, dressed in their pajamas, Kristy and Mary Anne set the box on the kitchen table and examined each picture.

"Kristy," Mary Anne said, "you have to tell your mom."

Kristy shook her head. "I can't. I promised. And you can't tell anyone."

"But I tell Dawn everything. And I tell Logan even more."

"You can't. Not this time, Mary Anne. Swear?"

"All right." Mary Anne offered Kristy her pinky. Kristy wrapped hers around it. "But who cares if he has a job or not?"

Kristy sighed. "Him, I guess. Can you believe when he gave me the dress? What was I supposed to say, 'Sorry, I only wear dresses at weddings and funerals'? He'd think I was crazy."

"You are," Mary Anne replied. Leafing through the photos, she smiled. "You look like him."

"What if I talk about him in my sleep?" Kristy asked.

"Don't worry. I'll stuff a pillow in your face."

Kristy stood up from the table and walked to the window. "I'm kind of freaked out by this."

With a clatter of footsteps, David Michael

and Karen ran into the kitchen. "Karen said I had to let my pet bugs go," David Michael complained.

"He has them under the bed," Karen reported. "It's not hygienic. Is it, Kristy?"

"I could wash them," David Michael suggested.

"Ask Watson if you can put your bug jar in his garden," Kristy said.

Karen peered at the photos on the table. "How come I'm not in these pictures?"

"Because it's from before my mom married your dad," Kristy explained.

David Michael pointed to a photo of Patrick. "Who's that man?"

"Your dad," Kristy replied.

"Oh." David Michael turned and ran toward the back door. "I'm going to sleep in Watson's garden."

Karen followed behind him. "A garden is not for people to sleep in. It's for flowers. That's why it's called a flower*bed*."

Kristy watched them through the kitchen window. She envied David Michael. He didn't remember.

He didn't feel a thing.

CHAPTER 10

"So, what do you think?" Claudia asked brightly.

As she, Kristy, Mallory, Dawn, Jessi, and Stacey walked around the greenhouse walls, they peeked through jagged holes in the grimy windows. The sunlight illuminated the rubble within. Trash was strewn among piles of brick and stone, and an old bird's nest or two had fallen from the dusty rafters.

It was a Thursday morning, and Claudia had insisted the members of the BSC examine the greenhouse before camp began.

Mallory pushed aside a vine to see the building's cornerstone. "It was originally built in 1767," she read.

"Did we even have a country back then?" Claudia asked.

"We checked into it," Dawn said. "It's owned by the town. But the civic committee said that if we fix it up and they approve it, we can use it."

The girls walked around and stepped through the open rear doorway.

"It's awfully dirty," Stacey remarked.

"It's really cool," Kristy said.

Stacey shook her head. "It kind of seems like a lot of work."

"We can get the kids into it," Claudia suggested. "One big arts and crafts project."

"You know how kids love dirt," Mary Anne said. "We can have a mud day."

Jessi grimaced. "It's hot in here."

Kristy pointed to a corner. "Meeting table over here, phone banks over there. Don't you think this would make an absolutely amazing office?"

Claudia raised an eyebrow and looked sharply at Kristy. "Yeah, I do. That's why I *suggested* it."

After camp that day, the girls walked to a shady area by the side of the barn. The late July sun had taken its toll.

"I'm wiped," Stacey said.

"Dead," Claudia agreed.

"Stace, how was your date with Luca?" Mary Anne asked.

Stacey smiled. "Smashing."

" 'Smashing'?" Kristy repeated. "Did he hit you over the head with his charm?"

Giggling, they all collapsed into the piled-up hay bales that lay against the barn wall.

"You guys," Mallory said, "my parents said we can use my aunt's lake cabin for Kristy's birthday party."

"Great!" Mary Anne exclaimed.

"Oh, Kristy, Watson told my stepdad he had some info on the greenhouse," Dawn said. "Did you bring it?"

"Uh, no," Kristy replied sheepishly. "I forgot."

I forgot were two words rarely heard from the mouth of Kristy Thomas. The girls were surprised.

"How could you forget?" Jessi asked.

"That's not like you, Kristy," Claudia said.

It's because I have more important things on my mind, Kristy wanted to say. Instead, she scowled and turned away.

The next morning, Cokie, Bebe and Grace spied on the BSC summer camp. From behind the hedges, Cokie whispered to Bebe and Grace, "Okay, you know what you're supposed to do. I'll distract them."

The two girls giggled. Clutching a stink bomb, Bebe led Grace around the side of the house.

Cokie could hear faint sounds of classical music from next door. There, Mrs. Haberman was feeding her birds while listening to the radio. *There's Mary Anne in a few years*, thought Cokie with a smirk.

She stood up and sauntered casually into the camp.

"I like your jeans, Logan," she sang out. "Nice fit."

"Cokie, how *are* you?" Mary Anne said sweetly through clenched teeth. "Your skin looks a little . . . dry."

"You're trying to insult me," Cokie replied. "How hilarious."

She gave Logan a squeeze on his biceps and walked off. His face began turning shades of red as Mary Anne glowered at him.

Cokie met her friends on the sidewalk, out of sight of the camp. They were beaming with pride.

"We planted it under a bush," Bebe announced.

"Great," Cokie said. "Did it break open?"

"We didn't break anything," Grace replied proudly.

Cokie's smug expression vanished. *"You were supposed to break it, you freak!"*

Nicky Pike was the lucky one who discovered the intact stink bomb. He brought it straight to his friends.

Emmy, Jonas and Daniel prepared the slingshot.

SPROIIIING!

As the bomb hurtled over the fence, Mrs. Haberman was planting bulbs in her garden. She saw it land on the ground and crack open.

Gasping with horror, she picked it up and threw it back.

The smoke made a wispy gray arc as the bomb landed at Kristy's feet.

"Yeeeeuuuuuch!" screamed the campers, running away.

"Cokie," Logan said, pinching his nose.

Jessi nodded. "Can we kill her?"

"It would be a mercy killing," Mallory replied.

As the smoke cleared, Kristy realized she had to leave camp early to meet her dad for a late lunch.

"What do you mean, you have to go?" Jackie protested, clutching his baseball bat. "We have to practice!"

"Jackie, I'm sorry," Kristy said. "How about tomorrow?" She jogged away, calling out, "Mallory, cover for me, okay? I have to leave!"

Mallory was in the music area, helping Jessi

choreograph a dance. She couldn't believe Kristy was leaving. Today the greenhouse cleanup was to begin. How could Kristy miss it? She sighed and went back to work.

"I shaved off my brother's eyebrow," Suzi said to Jessi.

"That's nice," Jessi replied.

Suzi turned toward Jessi's younger sister, Becca. "My sister has a nose on top of her head."

"That's nice," Becca said.

Stacey's eyes narrowed. Ahead of them, a man she didn't recognize was opening the door of a van for Kristy. Before climbing in, Kristy gave him a kiss.

"Who's that man?" Claudia asked.

"Is he a spy?" Jessi wondered.

"Is she in trouble?" Mallory said.

"Kristy has a *boyfriend*?" Stacey blinked, as if seeing a mirage.

"The world must be flat," Claudia muttered.

"Who's the guy?" Stacey asked.

"No one."

Everyone fell silent at Mary Anne's reply. They all turned to face her.

"*No one?*" Jessi repeated.

"Who is he, Mary Anne?" Dawn insisted.

"I can't say anything!" Mary Anne sputtered. "I promised."

Stacey raised her eyebrows. "Since when are we keeping secrets?"

At that moment, walking across her lawn toward the girls was Mrs. Haberman. She was smiling tightly, and still coughing from the smoke of the stink bomb.

"Hello," she called out. "I'm Emily Haberman? I live next door?"

"Oh, hi, Mrs. Haberman," Dawn said.

As Mrs. Haberman continued, her voice grew louder. "The first day I was assaulted by a jelly doughnut, which I was willing to ignore. Then, when my birds were disturbed, I turned the other ear. But just now, I was nearly asphyxiated by a stinky, smelly, disgusting projectile, and I frankly have had enough!"

"Gosh, we're sorry — " Claudia began.

Mrs. Haberman cut her off. "You look like decent, sensible girls, so we'll call this a warning. But if there's any more trouble — "

"There won't be," Dawn promised.

"Be sure of it," Mrs. Haberman snapped. "Because if there is, I'll talk to the city about revoking your permit."

With that, she walked back into the house.

The girls turned toward one other, dumbfounded.

"Permit?" they said in unison.

Hidden among the bushes, Cokie and her friends had heard the whole conversation.

"She's a *hermit*?" Grace whispered.

"Isn't that some kind of animal?" Bebe asked.

"*Permit*, you idiots!" Cokie hissed.

Quietly, the three girls tiptoed away.

Cokie couldn't believe her good luck. The Baby-sitters Club was dead meat.

CHAPTER 11

"How do I look?" Stacey ran down the stairs and stood in front of her mom in the entrance hall.

Any minute now, Luca was going to pick her up. Nothing fancy, he had said. Just hanging out. To get the right just-hanging-out - on - a - summer - day - with - the - world's - most-gorgeous-guy look, Stacey must have tried on forty-three outfits. Her arms were numb from the work. She felt weak and nervous.

"I think you look great," Mrs. McGill replied, looking at Stacey with concern. "Did you eat?"

"I will before I go," Stacey replied.

"Stace," Mrs. McGill said patiently, "if you eat on schedule and give yourself your insulin shots on time, your diabetes won't be a problem. If you don't — "

"I know, Mom!" *Whoa, calm down,* Stacey

had to remind herself. "I'm just nervous about Luca, that's all."

Ding-dong!

At the sound of the doorbell, Stacey stiffened.

Mrs. McGill nodded. "Yeah, so am I."

Stacey ran to the door and pulled it open. "Hi!"

Luca was wearing old khakis and a bandanna around his neck. A canteen was strapped to his belt. "You look smashing," he said.

"Thanks," Stacey replied. "So do you."

"I thought we'd go for a hike."

Stacey's smile wavered. "A . . . hike?"

"You do hike?" Luca asked.

"Hike? Sure. Love it. Do it all the time. Let me just tell my mom." Stacey turned back into the hallway. "Mom, we're going hiking. Okay, 'bye."

She grabbed her shoulder bag off the floor and started out the door.

"A hike? You? In that?" Mrs. McGill said, running toward the door. When she saw Luca, she smiled. "You must be Luca. I'm Stacey's mother, Maureen."

"It's a pleasure to meet you," Luca said.

"You need to eat something," Mrs. McGill reminded Stacey.

"I just had a muffin." Stacey shot her mother a Look. If she mentioned anything about diabetes, Stacey would die.

"Schuss!" Luca said cheerfully.

"Schuss, Mom," Stacey said, pulling Luca out the door.

Mrs. McGill watched them jog toward the sidewalk. *"Schuss?"* she said under her breath.

Stacey grabbed a branch to steady herself. Luca was scampering up the wooded hill ahead of her like a mountain goat, talking a mile a minute about the band he played in.

From the bottom, the hill hadn't seemed too steep. But Stacey was already feeling tired and winded.

Luca turned to wait for her. "If we keep going," he said, "we'll find it."

"Find what?" Stacey asked.

"Heaven," he said, flashing that melt-your-heart grin.

Stacey smiled wanly.

Luca took her hand. "You doing all right?"

"What?" The woods seemed to tilt a moment. "Oh, great."

"Good. Anyway, our band is called The Dogs. We're pretty good, if I do say so myself."

"I'd . . . love to see you play." Stacey's

vision blurred. She felt a chill. "Have you ever performed here? Oh, of course not, because you've never been here. . . ."

"Stoneybrook will be our first stop," Luca said with a laugh. "Come on. I heard there's a fantastic view at the top."

The top? Stacey took a deep breath and concentrated hard. Perspiration dripped coldly down her forehead. The trees were turning into greenish blobs. She blinked to clear her vision.

It seemed like a decade before they emerged into a clearing that overlooked the valley. Luca stopped and gazed around. "Isn't it wonderful up here?"

Stacey lost her footing and bumped into him. "Sorry."

Luca chuckled. "No, I love when you push me around."

"I'd better go home now." Stacey's voice was faint and hoarse.

Luca's smile vanished. "Are you okay?"

"I hate hiking!" Stacey suddenly exploded. "It was stupid of me to come."

"Well, why didn't you just say something?"

"Just go ahead on your stupid hike." Stacey turned away from Luca, blinking her eyes furiously. "I can find my way back."

Holding onto branches and tree trunks, she began to jog back.

Downhill was much easier. Stacey let her legs move as fast as they could. The woods seemed to speed by her, like a rear projection. Now even the sounds were muffled. Why was it becoming so dark? Was it late?

Stacey had a vague sensation of falling. Her eyes shut, and she could hear her heart beating.

"Stacey!" came Luca's distant voice. "What are you so angry about?"

She heard his footsteps pounding through the underbrush, coming nearer. Then they abruptly stopped.

"Stacey?"

Stacey's eyes flickered open. She was on the ground. She could feel a coating of sweat like a warm, suffocating bodysuit. "Luca . . ." she managed to whisper. "I need . . . something to eat . . ."

With that, her body went limp.

CHAPTER 12

Kristy cradled the telephone receiver on her shoulder as she packed snacks and drinks in a paper bag. Why did Claudia have to call just as she was leaving?

So much was racing around in Kristy's head. She needed to remember about five million things to tell her dad when she saw him.

"I'm sorry, Claud," Kristy said. "Can we do it tomorrow?"

"You promised to help me study, Kristy!" Claudia replied. "What's up with you?"

Kristy thought fast. "Um . . . it's David Michael's birthday and I have to be with my family. I'll make it up to you, I promise. 'Bye."

Click.

Tossing the paper bag into her backpack, Kristy headed for the kitchen door.

Her mom bustled in, carrying Emily Michelle. "Kristy," Mrs. Brewer said, "I'm going to the nursery to pick up the rosebushes. Come with me."

Ugh. Kristy's mind went into warp speed. "I have to go to Claudia's and help her study," she said.

"Oh, well, I'll take you," her mom replied. "It's on the way."

"Mmmm . . . I don't have to be there yet, so I was going to make myself a sandwich."

Mrs. Brewer nodded. "Okay. Let me take Emily Michelle upstairs to Nannie, and I'll join you."

"Oh. Umm . . . well, I was just going to take it with me, so I'll see you later!"

Kristy's mom left the kitchen, shaking her head in confusion.

Kristy bolted out the back door.

She raced into the garage, grabbed her bike, and pedaled away. The baseball field was on the other side of town, near Mary Anne's. It would be a long ride, and Kristy had one stop to make on the way.

When she reached the old greenhouse, she left her bike in the bushes and ran inside. Quickly, hidden by the debris, she pulled her neatly folded dress out of her backpack and changed into it.

Shoving her clothes into the pack, she ran back to her bike and pedaled all the way to the ball field.

She didn't have to wait too long for Patrick's van to pull up. When he emerged with a bat, a ball, and two mitts, she broke into a smile. Of all the things she'd missed about her dad, playing ball was top of the list.

"Nice dress," Patrick greeted her.

"Thanks," Kristy replied. "Hey, I know this apartment you could get. It's got a fireplace. I could make you chili. It's the only thing I know how to make. Do you like chili?"

"Love it," Patrick answered.

"And you could come watch me coach," Kristy went on. "There's this kid, Jackie Rodowsky? He's a total klutz, but there's something really special about him. And Matt, he's deaf, but we all sign, so there's no problem. Hey, maybe you could write about Kristy's Krushers in your column."

"Absolutely. How's that rocket arm of yours?"

Kristy grinned. She grabbed the bat and ran to home plate. Patrick put on his mitt and strode onto the pitcher's mound.

"Nineteen seventy-eight," Patrick intoned. "Yankees versus the Red Sox."

"One game playoff," Kristy added.

"Goose Gossage pitching."

"Carl Yastrzemski batting."

"It's a staredown between Gossage and Yastrzemski. Gossage winds up . . . he delivers . . ."

Patrick pitched the ball to Kristy. Kristy drew back the bat and swung.

With a loud *crrrack*, the ball shot over Patrick's head and into the outfield. Kristy took off, pumping her arms into the air. *"The Yaz hits it out of the park!"*

"That's not what happened!"

"It is this time!"

Patrick ran to first base, trying to cut her off. Kristy darted out of the way. "You can't obstruct a base runner!"

Patrick frowned. "Oh, yeah. You're right."

With a sudden lunge, he lifted her up and carried her back to home plate. Kristy giggled all the way.

A few blocks away, Claudia sat numbly in her summer school classroom. As her teacher sauntered up and down the aisle, handing out the graded quizzes, she felt faint. All she could think about was the box of Goobers she had stashed in her shoulder bag.

She closed her eyes as her paper was placed face down on her desk. She waited for her stomach to stop doing gymnastics, then opened her eyes and turned over the sheet.

Written on top in red was the letter *F*.

Claudia almost died.

CHAPTER 13

Crunch. With each bite of apple, Stacey felt better. She could practically feel her weakened blood soaking up the sugar in the apple.

How stupid could she have been? What would she have done if Luca hadn't brought food?

"Sorry," she said, shaking her head. "It's just that when my blood sugar gets low I get kind of psycho."

Luca nodded. "I wish you had told me you were diabetic. It's no big deal."

"Maybe not for you, but it makes people treat me like a kid. My mom is so overprotective. It makes me crazy worrying about her worrying about me."

"It's okay. I'm just glad you're better."

"I didn't want you to think I was sick or something. Or weird."

"I don't think you're weird," Luca said. "I think you're beautiful. *More* than beautiful. You're strong, and gentle, and full of light. . . ."

Luca leaned toward her. He drew his lips closer to hers.

Stacey closed her eyes. She was feeling weak again. But this time, she wasn't worried. She knew exactly what was happening.

Luca's kiss was sweet enough to last her a long, long time.

Sunburned and a bit dusty, Kristy and her dad wolfed down lunch by the side of the lake in Miller's Park.

"You look so grown-up," Patrick remarked.

Kristy tugged at the sleeves of her dress. "I feel like a pencil."

"You don't look like one." Patrick unwrapped a sandwich and took a big bite. "Mmmm, peanut butter and banana, my favorite!"

He turned to her and grinned, showing his mush-smeared teeth.

Kristy burst out laughing. "Dad? When you got here, you said you'd hear about your job in a couple of days. Now it's been a couple of weeks. When will you know?"

"Soon. Real soon." He dug some grapes out of the lunch bag and draped them around his ears. "Personally, I like grapes with my meal."

"You're so silly," Kristy said.

"Thank you," Patrick replied.

"I'm glad you're back."

Patrick put an arm around her, and they watched a swan take off from the quiet lake.

When Claudia's clock flashed 6:00 that evening, Kristy's chair was still empty.

Stacey looked out the window. No one had officially begun the meeting, and now it was almost over. "Kristy's never missed a meeting," she said.

"She did once. Her dog died," Jessi defended her.

"We've been waiting half an hour," Claudia said. "Let's start."

"I know I'm the alternate, but I'm beat," Dawn complained. "I think my potassium is down."

Claudia stood up from the bed, then sat in Kristy's chair. Taking a deep breath, she announced, "I call this meeting to order, since Kristy obviously has better things to do — "

Kristy suddenly barged in, still wearing her dress. "Hi, guys," she said. "Sorry I'm late."

"Kristy! You're wearing a dress!" Jessi remarked.

"Who died?" asked Mallory.

Kristy just smiled and shrugged. "Should we start?"

"We already have," Claudia said sharply.

"Okay, new business! The Mrs. Haberman problem."

Kristy sat in Claudia's place on the bed. "Who's Mrs. Haberman?"

"Oh, that's right, you missed that one," Dawn replied. "She's our neighbor, who is going to report us to the city and take away our permit for the camp."

"We don't need a permit," Kristy said. "I checked it out."

"It would have been nice if you had been there to tell her that," Stacey commented.

"I had an appointment," Kristy explained.

"Since when is a date an appointment?" Claudia asked.

"It wasn't a date!" Kristy insisted. "Look, Claudia, I said I'm sorry. I'll talk to Mrs. Haberman. It's no big deal."

"It is a big deal, Kristy," Mary Anne said.

Dawn nodded. "We could lose the camp."

"I said I'd handle it, okay?" Kristy shot back.

"Look, guys." Stacey stood up. "I have to go meet Luca."

As she left the room, Jessi rose to her feet. "I have to sit for Becca now."

"Let's go, Mary Anne," Dawn urged. "The Newtons are coming for dinner."

The sisters left, and Mallory followed, saying she had to go finish a novel.

Kristy exhaled and looked across the empty

room to Claudia. "Heard you flunked a quiz. Sorry."

"I'll bet you are," Claudia grumbled.

"There's still time. I'll help you."

"Yeah, I'll count on it."

"Claud, come on," Kristy pleaded.

"It's like you're not with us, Kristy."

Kristy nodded. "I know," she said quietly. "I will be." She stood up and slung her pack over her back. "Well, thanks for starting the meeting for me, Claud."

"Uh-huh."

"See you."

Steaming, Claudia watched Kristy leave. "Thanks for getting all the supplies, Claud," she murmured under her breath. "Thanks for dealing with Mrs. Haberman, Claud. Thanks for saving my butt, Claud."

She leaned over to her wall calendar. She crossed off the day, then circled the date of her final exam in bright red marker.

It was less than two weeks away. Two weeks to learn a course she'd been taking since last September.

Right.

CHAPTER 14

It was lunchtime. The campers were swapping sandwiches. Jamie Newton placed a Band-Aid on a broken potato chip. Margo Pike, who had carefully peeled a banana with her feet, placed it between her toes and offered it to Suzi.

"My mom's ears are longer than her arms," said Suzi, ignoring the banana.

Margo passed it to her sister. Vanessa Pike, who was nine, loved to speak in rhymes. "I don't eat bananas from feet," she said, "because they taste icky, not sweet like a treat."

As Alan passed by, Margo held out her foot to him.

"For me?" Alan said, removing the banana from her toes. "Thanks."

As he looked for Dawn, he spotted Jessi taking care of Jonas, who was barfing all over the lawn.

He smiled. *Kids*, he thought, taking a big bite of his banana.

Kristy ran by Alan, paying him no attention. She went straight to Mary Anne and pulled her away from a group of lunching kids.

Taking her arm, Kristy walked Mary Anne in the direction of the first-aid tent. "Last night at dinner I practically told my mom and Watson — twice!" Kristy whispered. "I don't know how long I can do this."

"How long is your dad going to be, you know, *not* here?" Mary Anne asked.

Kristy could sense the curious eyes of BSC members following them. "I have to help Claudia with her biology," she said, ducking into the tent.

Inside the tent, Claudia was sitting on a cot with her textbook. Kristy sat next to her.

"All right," Claudia said, "so, oxygen's kind of white, so it would be in the white blood cells, and corpuscles are kind of like blood, and blood's red, so it would be in the red cells. Right, Kristy?"

Kristy was lost in her own thoughts. "Huh?"

"You're not listening to me!" Claudia declared.

"No, I am. What did you say?"

"Like I can remember," Claudia said flatly. "Kristy, you know, you're not helping here."

"I know, I'm sorry. Look, Claudia, I'm just — I have so many things going on right now, my head hurts. Can we do this tomorrow?" Kristy stood up and walked toward the tent entrance.

"Wake up, Kristy!" Claudia said. "If I fail, I'm going to have to quit the club. But maybe that's what you want!"

Kristy turned around again. She could see the other BSC members gathering at the tent flap, listening. "Look, I'm sorry, okay?" she said.

"That's not good enough!" Claudia retorted.

"She said she — " Mary Anne began.

"Stay out of this, Mary Anne!" Claudia interrupted. "Kristy, I can't do your work and my work, too."

"I never asked you to," Kristy replied.

"Yes, you did!"

"Are we fighting?" Mallory piped up. "We never fight."

The tent fell silent. Outside, the campers were sounding restless.

Kristy stalked out the entrance. The others followed, one by one.

Mary Anne had salad duty that night at dinner. As she shredded lettuce, Dawn walked into the kitchen and opened a cupboard.

"Want some tahini?" she asked.

"I'll pass, thanks," Mary Anne replied.

Dawn pulled out a jar of tahini and some crackers. "What's going on with you and Kristy?"

"Nothing."

"It doesn't look like nothing," Dawn said hotly. "You're always whispering — "

"Do you think I should get my ears pierced?" Mary Anne asked.

"Don't change the subject."

Mary Anne took a deep breath. "Please don't be mad at me, okay? I'd tell you if I could, I swear. But I promised Kristy."

"Well, go be *her* sister, then!"

Leaving her food on the counter, Dawn stormed out.

All the next day, Mary Anne was on the verge of tears. Dawn hadn't spoken a word to her since the argument.

It was a greenhouse cleanup day for the camp. Logan's parents were friends with the local glass company owners, and they had agreed to replace the broken greenhouse panes for free.

Mary Anne spotted Kristy glancing at her watch, then telling Jessi she had to leave. Another appointment with her dad, no doubt.

Watching Kristy go, Mary Anne felt anger

and sadness and confusion. All this sneaking around was tearing apart the club, not to mention her home life. When was it going to stop?

Logan was walking closer to her as he squeegeed windows. "Hey, I got this new Ace of Base CD," he said. "Want to come over tonight and check it out?"

"Maybe tomorrow," Mary Anne replied.

Logan's cheerful expression disappeared. "Hey, Mary Anne, what's wrong?"

Mary Anne thought for a moment. "Logan," she finally said, "what would you do if a really good friend told you a secret, and you gave your word not to tell, but you were really worried about her?"

"Kristy?" Logan guessed.

Mary Anne nodded.

"I could tell something was up," Logan said. "But I didn't want to make you feel worse by bugging you."

"Tell that to my girlfriends, would you?"

Logan smiled, gave Mary Anne a kiss, and went on working.

Mary Anne watched Claudia and a few campers hang a banner painted with the words *Future Home of the Baby-sitters Club* across the front door.

From a branch of a nearby tree, Cokie and her friends peered between the leaves. Cokie smirked as she read the sign. "Awwww, they found a new home. What do you say we give them a housewarming party?"

"A party?" Grace repeated.

"Why do we want to throw them a party?" Bebe asked.

Cokie rolled her eyes. "I'm trading you guys in."

After camp, as parents arrived, Claudia grabbed her textbook and sat on a bench to study. But it was useless. She could not concentrate.

She looked up as Mary Anne passed by, carrying art supplies to the barn. "I can't believe my final's coming up so fast," Claudia complained. "If I fail, my life is ruined."

Mary Anne sat next to her. "You won't fail."

"What's the point of planning a big birthday party for her," Claudia continued, "when she probably won't even be there?"

"She'll be there," Mary Anne reassured her.

Across the campgrounds, David Michael ran to Jessi. "Where's Kristy?"

"She had to leave," Jessi replied. "Can I help?"

"Jessi!" Mallory called out, rushing to her

86

with Nina. "Nina can't find Jimmytony, and she said you know where he is."

Jessi smiled patiently and took Nina's hand. "Hold on, David Michael," she said. "I'll be right back."

David Michael frowned. He looked around the camp, but Kristy was nowhere to be seen. And he had to be home in time for dinner or his mom would be angry. Maybe Kristy had just forgotten.

He turned away from camp and began walking home alone.

Later that evening, Patrick dropped Kristy off a half block from her house.

Kristy waved to him until he drove out of sight. She practically skipped up the block to her house. She couldn't stop smiling.

Patrick was cool. No two ways about it. Flaky, but cool. Soon she'd be able to drop the sneaking around. Soon he would be settled in Stoneybrook for good.

Life was going to be perfect.

"Hi!" she called out, walking through the front door.

She breezed past the living room but stopped short when she saw the expressions on her parents' faces.

The twin masks of Anger and Fury. Crime and Punishment.

"Where were you?" were the first words from her mom's mouth.

"I, uh, had to pick up some things for camp," Kristy replied.

"Well, you forgot to pick up something pretty important," Mrs. Brewer shot back. "Like your brother."

Kristy felt the blood draining from her face. "Is he okay?"

"He tried to walk home by himself," Mrs. Brewer said. "I don't want to think about what would have happened if Mr. Kishi hadn't found him and brought him home."

Kristy was horrified. "Mom, I really am — "

"I can't talk to you right now." Seething, Mrs. Brewer stormed out of the room.

"Kristy, I can't believe you let this happen," Watson said. "What were you thinking?"

"It was a mistake, okay?" Kristy retorted.

"A very dangerous mistake. I don't understand what's gotten into you lately."

"That's right, you don't understand. You *wouldn't* understand."

"Understand what? Tell me! It's not like you to be this irresponsible! I'm your father and I want to know what's going on with you."

"You're not my father!" The words exploded out of Kristy's mouth. She turned, ran upstairs to her room, and slammed the door behind her.

CHAPTER 15

Stacey exhaled with frustration. Her mom was sitting at the desk in the entrance hall, calmly checking her mail, treating Stacey as if she were an annoying toddler.

What was so awful about going to New York? She'd done it plenty of times before.

"Dad wants me to visit him," Stacey said, "and Claudia could come with me. And you like Luca. So why can't we all go to New York?"

Mrs. McGill looked up. "After that little number you pulled on the hike? No way, Stace."

"Mom, give me a chance. Ever since you and Dad got divorced, you've been all over me. You don't give me a chance to take care of myself, because you're too busy doing it for me!"

Mrs. McGill sighed. "I'll think about it. Okay?"

As she turned back to the mail, Stacey grinned. *I'll think about it* was ninety percent of the fight.

Yes. It was going to happen!

At the Brewer house, Kristy huddled in the kitchen, speaking softly to her dad on the phone. Tears trickled down her face. "It's hard. Claudia flunked a quiz, and I was supposed to help her — "

"Who are you talking to, your boyfriend?" David Michael taunted, running into the kitchen.

"David Michael, your sister's on the phone," Watson scolded as he walked in and headed for the refrigerator.

"No, uh, there's a lot going on here all of a sudden," Kristy said into the receiver. "I'll have to call you back. . . . I will. . . . Okay, 'bye."

She hung up.

"Everything okay?" Watson asked.

"Yeah, fine," Kristy said.

"You sure? Who were you talking to?"

"Nobody."

Now Mrs. Brewer entered the kitchen. "Kristy, what's wrong? Are you crying?"

"Could everybody just leave me alone?" Kristy said. "It's an allergy attack, that's all!"

"What are you allergic to?" David Michael asked.

"Summer," Kristy said.

At the end of the next day's lunch, Alan walked over to the compost heap, where Dawn and the campers were throwing away apple cores and watermelon rinds.

He sniffed deeply. "Mmm, I love the smell of compost in the morning."

Dawn couldn't help but giggle.

"Hey, Dawn, you look really pretty," Alan said with a grin. "And I love what you're doing for the environment."

Dawn felt herself blushing. "Well, thanks, Alan."

He bounded away past the music area, flapping his arms like they were wings. Some of the campers followed him. Dawn could only shake her head.

As Kristy arrived at camp the next day, a few carloads of campers were being dropped off. She walked toward the other BSC members, who were standing in a group and talking.

"It's so cool your folks are letting us use the cabin," she heard Jessi say to Mal.

"Yeah," Mallory replied. "And my mom's

going to drive us out, too — and she promised she'd keep my brothers out of the way."

"Kristy's going to have the best birthday," Jessi said.

"I don't know if she deserves it," Claudia grumbled.

As Kristy drew nearer, Stacey changed the subject. "Luca asked me to go to New York with him."

"Yyyyyes!" Claudia said.

"Who-o-o-oa!" Jessi whooped.

"Are you going to go?" Dawn asked.

"I don't know. My mom said I could if it's okay with my dad. I think she might let me." Stacey grinned slyly. "If Claudia comes with me."

"Me?" Claudia shook her head. "I can't. I have to study. The test is next week. If I live that long."

Stacey looked at Dawn. Dawn looked at Mary Anne. Mary Anne grinned. "As long as you live a few more minutes, I think you'll be okay."

Suddenly Logan and Alan appeared from nowhere and sang a fanfare: "Da-da-da-daaa-aah!"

Mallory, Jessi, and Dawn began rounding up campers.

"What's going on?" Claudia asked.

"Today," Kristy announced, "using the BSC quick-study method, you're going to learn about the human body!"

"Don't bother," Claudia said. "I'm not interested."

"Does the Baby-sitters Club interest you?" Mallory asked.

"It's my life!" Claudia retorted.

"Then get interested." Mallory darted onto the porch, where the staff and campers were now waiting.

Clap.

Stomp.

Clap.

Stomp.

Using their hands and feet, everyone began beating a rhythm. Claudia watched in bewilderment as they started rapping.

Yes, rapping.

They had planned it. Written it out. And the words of the rap were all the parts of the body Claudia needed to know about — the cerebral cortex, the cerebellum, the hypothalmus, all the chambers of the heart.

The song was hilarious, but also incredibly helpful. Claudia realized how much work had gone into it, how much caring. She didn't know whether to laugh or cry.

After the song was over, the members of the BSC lined up one by one to hand Claudia a favorite good luck charm.

Kristy was the last. She dug a pair of dirty shoelaces from her pocket and held them out to Claudia. "I was wearing them when I hit my first home run," she said.

"Thanks," Claudia said, beaming. "Thanks, guys. I can use all the help I can get."

CHAPTER 16

Kristy glanced at the kitchen clock. Half past seven. It was now the day of Claud's biology test. Claudia had been scheduled to baby-sit for the Barretts after the test, but she must be home by now.

Kristy poured herself a bowl of cereal, then tapped out Claudia's number on the phone.

"Hello?" said Claudia's voice.

"Hey, Claud, how'd the test go?"

"I think okay."

"Good! What are you doing?"

"Listen, Kristy, I can't talk now. I'll see you tomorrow, okay? 'Bye."

" 'Bye."

Click.

Just like that. End of conversation.

Kristy called Mary Anne.

"Hello?"

"Hey, Mary Anne. I — I just called Claudia, but she was kind of weird."

Kristy stared into her cereal. Her hunger had flown out the window. All she wanted to do now was cry. She knew why Claudia had been so cold. She had flunked. That had to be it.

And it's all my fault, Kristy said to herself.

"Are you okay?" Mary Anne asked.

"No. Not really. All this sneaking around — I feel like a rat."

"So do I," Mary Anne admitted. "They're ganging up on me, too, you know. And Dawn's practically not talking to me."

Kristy gazed out the kitchen window. Outlined by the evening light, her mom was picking tomatoes in the garden.

"If I tell the truth," Kristy said, "then I betray my dad. And if I don't, then I'm lying to my mom and friends."

"Well, you've already done that," Mary Anne said. "And you've got me doing it, too. I'll call you later."

Kristy said good-bye and hung up. She'd never heard Mary Anne sound so cold.

She stared at her cereal, which was slowly becoming a mushy, soggy lump. Just like her heart.

The back door opened and Mrs. Brewer walked in, holding an enormous tomato. "Kristy, look at Nannie's tomatoes. They're huge. Want to try one?"

"Okay." Kristy thought a moment. Maybe

her mom would understand. Maybe she should know the truth. "Mom?"

"Yes, sweetheart?"

Say it! a voice screamed inside Kristy.

"I . . . I . . ."

Her mother turned and looked at her.

"You've got some tomato on your chin," was all Kristy could bring herself to say.

The moment Jackie Rodowsky was dropped off at camp the next day, he ran to the BSC members and found Kristy. "Kristy, I hit one yesterday!"

"Jackie, that's incredible!" Kristy said.

"Well, I kind of hit one. It hit my bat and then kind of fell off. It might be the closest to a home run I'm ever going to hit in my life. And you didn't see it."

"Jackie, you're going to hit more," Kristy reassured him. "All you needed was to break the ice."

"Yeah . . ." he replied, slumping away sadly.

"You really let him down, Kristy," Claudia said.

"Give it a rest, Claud," Mary Anne snapped.

"No, Claudia's right," Dawn insisted. "What is up with you, Kristy?"

"You're always leaving early," Stacey said.

"You're acting so weird," Dawn added.

"Yeah," Mallory agreed.

"You have a responsibility here," Claudia said.

"You owe us," Jessi cut in.

Kristy's heart was pumping wildly. This was so strange. All of this scolding — all of their words — for so long, Kristy had been saying the same things to *them*! Of course they were right. Absolutely. And she wanted to tell them so, but it was impossible.

Kristy felt like a mouse in a trap.

"I can't tell you," she said weakly.

"But you can tell Mary Anne," Claudia said.

"She's my best friend!" Kristy protested.

In the stunned silence, Kristy turned and walked away.

That afternoon, Patrick drove Kristy to the minor league ballpark in a nearby town. Players were practicing on the field. Kristy knew Patrick had once played in the minors — maybe even for this team, the Comets. She tried hard to feel excited about that, but she couldn't.

As they walked through the bleachers, Patrick pointed to a graying, middle-aged coach. "I used to play ball with Mickey Woolen over there. Except the ballparks we played in had lights. You know, I wanted to take you with me on the road a couple of times, but your mom wouldn't let me."

Mickey Woolen waved to them. Patrick waved back, then put his arm around Kristy's shoulder.

Kristy felt herself stiffen.

"I hear you have a birthday next week," Patrick said.

"Yep," Kristy answered.

"Remember that birthday of yours when I took you to Monty's? I couldn't get you off the roller coaster. The only five-year-old who wasn't afraid of the Monster." He chuckled. "Hey, how about for your birthday, you and me go back there and ride the Monster until we puke?"

For an awful moment, Kristy realized who her dad reminded her of just then. "You sound like this kid, Alan, in my class. He's a real goofball and can be a major jerk."

Patrick looked stunned. "So you think I'm a jerk?"

"Well, you don't act like . . . a dad."

"And I guess Webster does," Patrick said.

"Watson," Kristy corrected.

"Watson."

"Kind of. Last week David Michael got lost, and it was my fault because I was with you. I thought Watson was going to kill me."

Patrick's eyes were focused on the game. "Sounds pretty rough."

"Yeah, but I messed up, big time, and he didn't let me off the hook."

"As long as you're okay with it." Suddenly Patrick called out at the top of his lungs: "Hey — nice catch — why don't you open your eyes next time!" With a disgusted sigh, he turned to Kristy. "Let's go get a hot dog."

Kristy started to follow him to the refreshment stand, then stopped. "Why'd you come back if you're just going to hide?"

Patrick turned. "I came back to see you. I missed you."

"You could have come before. Nothing was stopping you."

"I tried — "

"You sent two cards in, like, five years or something." The words were beginning to pour out now. Kristy couldn't hold them back. "I was always thinking you'd come, and you never did. Ever. I'd wait for you, every year. And you never even called! You don't care about me. And everyone who does care about me is mad at me. I can't do this anymore. I've never lied to Mom or my friends, and since you've been here, that's all I've been doing. I hate it, and it's all your fault! I'm going to tell Mom you're here."

"Kristy, I thought we had a deal."

"I'm breaking it. Just like you broke all your promises."

"I'm here, aren't I?" Patrick snapped. He took a deep breath and looked away. "Kristy, I'm sorry. I know I haven't been there for you. I know I can't change what's happened in the past, but I can sure do something about now. About you and me." He turned to face Kristy eye to eye. "When we go to Monty's on your birthday, I'm going to pick you up at home, and we can tell everyone the good news together. All right?"

"Really?"

Patrick wrapped Kristy in a big bear hug. "Absolutely."

Kristy squeezed tight. "That's the best present you could ever give me."

CHAPTER 17

Kristy's rag blackened as she wiped the rear window inside the greenhouse. Under the grime, the glass was green-tinted and beautiful.

"The place has to be squeaky-clean when the civic committee comes to inspect on Monday!" Dawn called out.

Mallory looked up from a bucket of suds. "Kristy, you're driving out with us for your party, right?"

"I might be a little late," Kristy replied, "but I'll be there. I've got my own ride."

"I can't breathe in here!" Jessi complained.

Stacey tried to open a window, then stopped. Her eyes fixed on an approaching figure. "It's Claud! I hope she passed."

Kristy raced to the greenhouse entrance. Dawn, Stacey, Mary Anne, Jessi, and Mallory gathered around her. They watched Claudia turn slowly up the walkway. Her eyes were cast downward, her mouth tight.

Kristy's heart was sinking.

Claudia walked closer and looked up.

Her face broke into a grin. "I got a B-minus."

Kristy thought the screams of joy would shatter the greenhouse glass. Her friends mobbed Claudia in a big group hug.

Kristy wanted to join in, but she felt awkward. Instead, quietly, she said, "Claud, that's the best news."

Claudia didn't know which was better: that she could still be part of the Baby-sitters Club, or that she could go with Stacey and Luca to New York.

On the train ride to the Big Apple, she could barely sit still. From Grand Central Station, they took a subway to Soho. Stacey practically had to drag Claudia away from the art galleries they walked past.

They met three of Luca's friends at a wild restaurant where just about everyone was dressed in black and had great hair. Ricky, Mark, and Brookes seemed about nineteen years old to Claudia. Brookes had strange, thick hair that sat on her head like a small house. All of them looked a little bleary-eyed and unsteady.

When Claudia saw Ricky pass a flask to Brookes, she knew why.

"Have you known Luca long?" Ricky asked as they sat down.

"Uh, awhile," Stacey replied.

Brookes's arm accidentally swiped a salt shaker off the table.

"Brookes!" Luca warned. "Maybe you should take it easy with that stuff."

Claudia asked, "How do you guys know each other?"

"We met in London," Mark replied.

"At school," Luca added. "They were exchange students."

"So, what are you guys studying?" Ricky asked.

"Science," Claudia answered. "I'm in summer school."

"Wow. You must be really boring, to study in the summer," Brookes remarked.

Claudia shrugged. "Well, I don't have much choice."

"Of course you have a choice," Mark spoke up. "Just don't go."

"If I didn't — " Claudia began.

"Uh, Claudia's studying anatomy," Stacey interrupted. "She's an artist."

"What's your major?" Claudia asked Brookes.

"Linguistics," she replied.

"Really?" Claudia brightened. "My sister cooks, too. She does hers with clam sauce."

Yikes. Stacey was cringing. Did Claudia intend to ruin the whole night? She began coughing loudly, hoping Claudia would get the hint.

Mark handed the flask to Stacey. "Here, take a shot."

"No, thanks," Stacey said.

"Oooh, yeah, you're right." Brookes was beginning to slur her words now. "You shouldn't drink. It might actually make you fun."

"Brookes, give Stacey a break. She's only sixteen." Luca flashed his smile Stacey's way. "A delicious sixteen."

Stacey couldn't help seeing the look of utter astonishment on Claudia's face.

After dinner, they took a cab to a dance club downtown. A broad-shouldered man stopped them at the door. "IDs," he said.

Luca and his friends reached into their pockets and took out driver's licenses. Stacey and Claudia tried to blend into the crowd that was entering behind them.

"Ladies?" the man said sternly.

Claudia and Stacey opened their shoulder bags and pulled out their wallets. "Oh, I must have left it in my other wallet," Stacey said.

"Come on, cut her a break," Luca pleaded to the man. "She's sixteen. They both are."

"It's right here!" Brookes took Stacey's wallet, opened it to an ID, and showed it to the man.

He peered at it and shook his head. "Sorry, babe. Nice try."

Luca was becoming angry. "Hey, come on. She showed you her ID."

"Yeah, I know," the man replied gruffly. "And she ain't no sixteen. So beat it."

"I'm almost . . . close to sixteen," Stacey squeaked.

As Luca grabbed the ID card from the man and looked at it, Stacey turned and ran. She was absolutely mortified.

Claudia caught up to Stacey down the block. When they looked back, they saw Luca's friends walking into the club. Luca was stalking toward Stacey and Claudia, his face tight-lipped and somber.

Wordlessly he hailed a cab. They piled in, Stacey first, then Claudia, then Luca.

As the car zipped silently uptown, Stacey wanted to melt into the seat cushion.

Finally Luca exploded. *"Thirteen?"* he yelled across the cab.

Claudia jumped in her seat.

"I can't believe you're only thirteen!"

"Can you stop screaming in my ear?" Claudia asked.

The cabdriver looked over her shoulder. "My husband and I were engaged when we were thirteen."

"You stay out of this," Luca snapped.

"Let me out here, please," Stacey called to the driver.

Luca's face was crimson. "I'm not about to let two thirteen-year-old girls — "

"Shut up!" Stacey screamed.

"You know, I thought maybe you weren't *quite* sixteen," Luca said. "But I never imagined you were *thirteen*! Let me tell you something. You've got some pretty weird notions about what's important. Diabetes is nothing, but this — *this is a really big deal!*"

Claudia covered her ears.

"Jerk," Stacey muttered.

"Oh, yeah, I'm a big jerk." Luca snorted a laugh. "I'm a jerk for getting mad because you lied to me!"

The cab stopped in front of Grand Central Station. It was the shortest visit to New York Stacey had ever had.

When Claudia and Stacey arrived back at the McGill house, they raced upstairs. Stacey collapsed in tears on her bed.

"I should be crying, too," Claudia said, sinking onto the bed next to her, "from the black-and-blue mark you gave me when you elbowed me at the table."

Stacey's response was a flurry of sobs.

"What's a linguistic, anyway?" Claudia asked.

Stacey choked back a sniffle and sat up. "Roots of language."

"Oh. I thought it was a spaghetti."

Stacey looked at Claudia. Claudia looked at Stacey.

That did it. Together, they broke into a fit of laughter.

"Brookes was scary," Claudia proclaimed. "And what about that hair? It looked like a building."

Stacey cackled hysterically until her laughs became gasps of crying. She flopped downward, burying her face in her pillow.

"If he really likes you," Claudia said soothingly, "it's not going to matter."

Stacey nodded in agreement. But inside, she didn't believe a word of it.

CHAPTER 18

"Flowers and dirt never make you hurt," recited Vanessa Pike.

She took a flower from a pile of uprooted plants. Then she and Suzi placed it into a hole beside the greenhouse. "My pants are from a bear," said Suzi.

"What kind of bear?" Becca challenged her.

"Alligators like to fly," Suzi answered.

Becca rolled her eyes. "That's nice."

The greenhouse looked like a new building. The campers scurried around, painting, cleaning, touching up. Finally, at the end of August, it was going to be finished.

And on Kristy's birthday, too, Dawn thought as she inspected the grounds. At any other time, that would have made her happy.

These days, she wasn't so sure.

She stopped to watch Suzi, Becca, and Vanessa. The flowers they were planting were gorgeous. And they looked familiar.

"Where'd you get those?" she asked.

"We picked them," Suzi replied.

"From where?"

"My South American zinnias!"

Mrs. Haberman's bellowing voice answered the question. She marched toward them, her face crimson. "My variegated columbine! My tithonia!"

"Mrs. Haberman, please calm down," Dawn said.

"Calm down?" Mrs. Haberman thundered. "These aberrations that you call children beheaded my precious flowers as if they were nothing more than — than *broccoli!*"

"We'll replace them," Dawn said. "I promise."

"Replace? Are you going to fly to Africa? You don't seem to understand. These flowers are royalty! I have had enough. I'm calling the city."

She turned and stomped away.

Dawn thought about the herbs she had been growing in her house. Maybe Mrs. Haberman would accept them, as kind of a peace offering. "Alan," she called out, "can you look after my group for a few minutes?"

Alan lit up. *"This* Alan?"

As Dawn ran off, Suzi announced. "I have little animals walking around in my pockets."

"Cool," Alan replied.

* * *

As Dawn approached Mrs. Haberman's house, she peeked at the garden and cringed. The damage was worse than she'd expected. It was a tangled mess of exposed roots and upturned soil.

She knocked on the door, and Mrs. Haberman answered.

"I'm so sorry, Mrs. Haberman," Dawn said, stepping inside. She held out her flowerpot. "I've been growing these since spring. They're only herbs, sage and rosemary, and I know it won't make up for what happened or replace your beautiful flowers. But they're delicious and they smell nice, and I would really like you to have them."

"You're right, they don't make up for it," Mrs. Haberman said curtly. "I planted those flowers especially for the hummingbirds and the butterflies. Your name again?"

"Dawn."

"How sixties." Mrs. Haberman gave a faint smile. "I do appreciate the gesture, Dawn."

"I think hummingbirds are magical. They look like little jewels."

Mrs. Haberman's expression softened. "Would you like some tea?"

"Sure."

As Mrs. Haberman went off to the kitchen, Dawn looked around the living room. It contained an odd assortment of furniture and art, all of it foreign and exotic.

She stopped in front of a group of framed photos. One showed a young woman in fatigues, with cameras slung around her neck. Next to it, the same woman was in hiking gear on top of a mountain.

Mrs. Haberman bustled into the room with a tea service and set it down on a table.

"Is that you in those pictures?" Dawn asked.

"Yes." Mrs. Haberman stood next to Dawn and picked up the two photos. "This one was in Vietnam. I spent a few years there taking pictures. This other one was when I was trekking in the Himalayas. That was a wonderful trip. We walked in the clouds."

"Wow." Dawn took a cup of tea and sipped. "Mmm, oatstraw. My dad and I used to drink this. He's still in California. That's where I grew up."

"There are some exquisite ruby-crowned kinglets in California," Mrs. Haberman said. "That is, if the pollution hasn't killed them by now."

"It was still pretty nice when I was there. I used to sit at the bottom of this one redwood tree all the time."

"And do what?"

"Nothing."

Mrs. Haberman nodded knowingly. "The

quiet can be a wonderful companion — one that I've missed lately.'' She gave Dawn a fond but exasperated look. "You're most delightful, Dawn, but I don't know how much more I can take.''

"Please, Mrs. Haberman, it's only for a few more days.''

"How many?''

Dawn swallowed. "I don't know.''

"Then I don't know, either," Mrs. Haberman said sharply.

Soon after Stacey arrived home from camp, Luca showed up on her front porch. From her second-floor bedroom she could hear his harmonica, then his knock on the door.

She clenched up. No way was she going to see him.

"Stacey," Mrs. McGill called up, "Luca's outside.''

Stacey ran downstairs. "Tell him I'm not here," she said.

"You'll feel a lot better if you go out there and talk to him," Mrs. McGill said.

"No, I won't.''

"Honey, he called six times. The least you could do is listen to what he has to say.''

Luca's mournful harmonica tune began again. Stacey and her mother fell silent and listened.

"He's pretty good on that thing," Mrs. McGill remarked.

Stacey sighed to herself. He was pretty good. For a jerk.

Claudia, Dawn, and Mary Anne had stayed on at the greenhouse with Alan and Logan. The steps to the entranceway had needed cementing, which had to be done after the campers left.

As the boys finished smoothing the wet cement, the girls began to leave.

"Shut the door on the way out, okay?" Claudia asked.

"Nice work, guys," Dawn commented.

As they walked away, Alan put down his trowel and watched Dawn. "She likes me," he said under his breath. "She really likes me."

Kristy's parlor clock clicked to five-thirty. She sneaked a glance out the window. Patrick's van was nowhere to be seen. He was supposed to have picked her up a half hour earlier. He always parked in the same place down the street, partially visible.

Where was he?

As she paced the floor, her mom walked briskly through the room. "Hey, birthday girl, when are your friends picking you up?"

"Soon," Kristy replied.

"I wish I were going to the lake," Mrs. Brewer said.

Kristy waited until her mom had gone into the next room. Then she picked up the phone and quietly tapped out the number of the Strathmore Inn. "Patrick Thomas, please," she whispered. "Are you sure? Did he leave a note or . . . Could you check again? . . . Uh-huh. . . . Thanks."

He was gone. Checked out. Could she have missed him? Had he been delayed? Had he driven straight to Monty's?

Kristy grabbed a sweatshirt that was lying around. She glanced into the living room, where her mom was playing the piano. Then she tiptoed out of the house.

She had enough money for a cab. She would meet him there.

CHAPTER 19

Mary Anne glanced at the sky outside the cabin window. Through the dark clouds, she couldn't see the setting sun. In the distance, the lake was choppy. She hoped it wouldn't rain.

To tunes blasting from Stacey's boom box, Mal and Jessi unfurled a banner that read *Happy Birthday, Kristy!* As they tacked it onto the wall, Dawn and Mary Anne spread a cloth on a folding table. Then Stacey and Claudia set out hot dogs, buns, marshmallows, chocolate, and pastries.

The girls sat, their excited faces illuminated by kerosene lanterns. "She should be here any minute," Mary Anne said, looking out the window.

"She's been late all summer," Claudia replied.

"Why is the cake melting?" Mallory asked.

The girls watched Kristy's birthday cake slump slowly southward.

Jessi shook her head in disbelief. "Who bought an *ice cream* cake?"

A distant rumble of thunder interrupted them. The girls gave each other nervous looks.

In the evening's fading light, Cokie and her friends approached the greenhouse. Cokie carried poles and shaving cream cans, Grace paint cans and toilet paper, and Bebe brushes and rollers.

BOOOOM!

Cokie jumped at the sound of thunder. "Gee, it looks like it's going to rain." As she turned toward Bebe, her pole smashed through a greenhouse window. "Whoops!"

Bebe and Grace exploded with laughter.

Setting some of the equipment down, the girls brought a paint can into the greenhouse through the back door. Cokie pried it open, and Bebe accidentally stuck her hand in the paint.

"Ewww!" Screaming with laughter, Bebe began putting handprints on the walls.

Within minutes, the pristine inner walls were covered. Now for the outside.

"There are more shaving cream cans around the side," Cokie said. "Get them and meet me by the front door."

Bebe and Grace ran out the back.

Cokie went through the front door. She yanked it open and placed her foot on the top step.

It sank into the drying cement. She couldn't move.

"Hand me the supplies!" Cokie shouted.

Grace and Bebe scurried toward her. *Shhhlurp*. They could go no farther than the bottom step.

"I'm stuck!" Bebe said.

"Me, too!" whispered Grace.

Grunting, Cokie tried to pull her foot out. It wouldn't budge.

Grace and Bebe howled with laughter.

Beyond the next-door fence, Mrs. Haberman was photographing nightbirds in the moonlight. In her telephoto lens, she noticed some movement in the greenhouse. She walked closer, focusing carefully. Soon she could make out exactly what was happening.

Rain began streaking Kristy's face. A flash of lightning bathed the amusement park in eerie white. Families were heading out to the parking lot in droves.

And there he was. Running toward the exit, his jacket pulled over his head.

"Dad!" Kristy called out. *"Daddy!"*

She ran to him and grabbed his arm. He whirled around toward her.

It wasn't Patrick. It was a stranger.

Kristy ran away. Tears fell from her eyes, stinging warm, running down her cheeks with the cold rain.

At a pay phone, she dug a quarter and a crumpled piece of paper out of her pocket. On it was the phone number of the cabin. She tapped out the number and waited.

"Hello, Mallory? I'm at the — hello? Hello?" *BOOOOOOM!*

The phone was dead. But Mallory had picked up. And Kristy knew her friends were with her. Waiting. Worrying.

No, maybe not worrying. At this point, they all probably hated her.

Kristy was shivering. She ran toward the nearest exit, but it was locked.

She circled the park. Each exit had been padlocked.

Where were the guards? Had they gone home?

As Kristy sprinted frantically, aimlessly, through the empty park, a bolt of lightning split the sky.

With growing panic, she realized she was locked in. She decided to climb over the fence.

CHAPTER 20

At the cabin, Mallory stared at the phone receiver. A dial tone buzzed faintly. "We got cut off."

"Where is she?" Dawn asked.

Mallory shrugged.

All eyes turned to Mary Anne.

She swallowed hard. "I promised . . ."

"Something horrible could have happened!" Dawn cried.

"We have to find her," Claudia added.

Mary Anne took a deep breath. "Kristy's dad came back. Her real dad."

Dawn, Stacey, Claudia, Mallory, and Jessi stared at her in shock. Suddenly the rain seemed to be pounding twice as hard on the roof.

"Is that who that guy was?" Mallory asked.

Mary Anne nodded.

"Wow," Jessi said.

"We have to call her mom," Claudia insisted.

"No," Mary Anne said. "Kristy made me swear. We can't tell anyone."

"We can't just sit here!" Dawn pleaded.

Stacey looked at Mallory. "When are your parents getting back?"

"Late," Mallory replied.

"We'd need a car to get to where Kristy is," Mary Anne said.

For a moment, no one said a word. Then Stacey ran to the phone and began tapping out a number.

"Hello, Luca?" she said.

When Luca arrived at the cabin, the girls piled into his car and he sped to Monty's.

At the front gate, they climbed out. A guard emerged from a small shack and walked toward them. "Park's closed," he said.

"Our friend's in there!" Mary Anne insisted.

The guard smirked. "Yeah, and it's going to start snowing any minute."

Suddenly a figure came running by the locked gate.

"Kristy?" Mary Anne cried.

In the beam of Luca's flashlight, Kristy's eyes were wide and frightened. Her hair was a tangled mat, her face drawn and tear-streaked. She blinked in confusion as her friends ran to her.

Mary Anne was the first to throw her arms around Kristy. Kristy was cold and shivering, her clothes soaked.

"Mary Anne!" Kristy gasped.

The park's entranceway echoed with joyous sobs. But none were louder than Kristy's.

She was making up for lost time.

At the cabin, Mary Anne, Dawn, Claudia, Jessi, and Mallory helped Kristy out of the car.

Stacey remained behind with Luca. "Luca," she said, "I know I've been a real nightmare. You probably can't wait to get back to London and hang out with all your friends."

"Stace — " Luca began.

"I just really wanted to get to know you," Stacey barged on. "I never met anyone like you. Anyway, that's why I did what I did."

"Are you finished?"

"Look, I know I went on way too long. I'm really sorry, I just wanted to get it out."

Luca leaned closer to her. "Stacey, I didn't tell you. I'm coming back next summer."

Stacey looked into his eyes and realized he wasn't angry. Far from it. "I'll be fourteen," she said hopefully.

"I know," Luca replied.

And he kissed her.

After Luca went home, Stacey joined the others by the fireplace, where Kristy was warming up, wrapped in a wool blanket.

"My life's a joke," Kristy said, her eyes welling up.

"I felt the same way when my mom and dad split," Stacey remarked.

Dawn nodded sympathetically. "Me, too. It's the worst."

"When my grandma Mimi died last year, I stayed in my room crying for two days," Claudia said. "I didn't think I'd ever feel good again."

Kristy sniffled. "I feel so stupid. I mean, I really believed him this time."

"It's not your fault, Kristy," Jessi insisted.

"I thought I was more important to him," Kristy went on.

"You're important to us," Mallory said.

Kristy tried to smile. "I screwed up the whole summer."

"Okay, so this summer was your turn," Stacey said with a shrug.

"I can't believe you guys are still talking to me," Kristy murmured.

Mary Anne looked warily at Dawn. "Are *you* still talking to *me*?"

"Only if I can borrow your plaid jacket for the rest of the year," Dawn replied.

Mary Anne's eyes misted over and she nodded.

Jessi and Mallory quietly stood up and left the room. Kristy wondered where they were going, but no one seemed to notice.

"Kristy," Claudia said, "I wouldn't have yelled at you if I'd known."

"Yes, you would've," Kristy replied.

Claudia thought about this for a moment. "Yeah, I guess I would've."

The room erupted with giggles.

A moment later Jessi and Mallory returned. Grinning from ear to ear, they held aloft a melted ice cream birthday cake with burning candles. "Make a wish!" they cried.

Kristy was beaming. She leaned forward and pulled the blanket around herself even tighter. She hadn't felt this warm in a long time.

Too long.

CHAPTER 21

Mrs. Brewer's face was ashen. She seemed to sink into her lounge chair as Kristy spoke.

It was the day after the storm. Kristy had been so tired when she arrived home the night before, she'd gone right to bed.

Now, on the Brewers' back patio, in the warmth of the morning sun, she had decided to tell her mom the entire story.

"I can't believe he was here for over a month, and you never told me," Mrs. Brewer said.

"You think I liked not telling you?" Kristy asked. "It was really hard."

"I'm sure it was hard, but that's no reason for lying."

"He made me promise."

"I'm sure he did."

"He said we were going to tell you on my birthday."

Mrs. Brewer shook her head angrily. "I

125

could just wring his neck for doing this to you."

"Maybe if I'd been different, he wouldn't have left."

"No, Kristy, you're not supposed to be the grown-up here. Your father says he's going to do a lot of things he doesn't do."

"Why is he like that?" Kristy asked.

"Oh, honey, I wish I knew. I believed him, too." Mrs. Brewer's eyes grew sad. She leaned toward Kristy and gave her a hug.

"I did have a really good time with him," Kristy said. "He made me laugh."

Mrs. Brewer nodded. "I know. That's one of the wonderful things about him. He loves you, you know."

"I guess it's just different from the way you and Watson love me."

"Here, this was in the mailbox," Mrs. Brewer said, pulling an envelope out of her pocket.

Kristy ripped it open and read aloud: " 'Dear Kristy, I want to tell you this in person, but I don't have the heart, or the guts, I guess. The job didn't work out. Can you believe it, after all that? Hope your birthday's great. Remember, I owe you a ride on the Monster. Love, Dad. P.S. I'm on my way to Colorado. Chris Almond told me there's an opening for a stringer on the paper there.' "

126

Colorado.

Kristy slumped. She folded the letter up.

Mrs. Brewer gave her a warm smile, sad but somehow reassuring. "Your dad's full of dreams, baby. So are you. That's not a bad thing."

The next day, Kristy and her friends walked to the greenhouse for final inspection.

When they saw it, they stopped short.

A fallen branch lay across the yard, blocking the front entrance. The banner had been torn down. The door was wide open. One of the windows was now jagged shards of glass. Walls had been plastered with shaving cream and toilet paper.

They walked around the building and entered through the back door. Inside, their mouths dropped open in shock.

The inner walls were a mess, too. It looked like a kindergarten project run amok.

"The civic committee is coming today," Mary Anne said under her breath.

"We're dead meat," Jessi replied.

Mallory was the first to see the shoes on the front steps.

Three pairs of shoes. Stuck in the cement.

"Hey, you guys," she called out. "It's like that thing in Hollywood."

The other BSC members peered around her. "Cokie melted," Jessi remarked.

"That girl," Dawn said, "is building up some very bad karma."

Kristy and Claudia went to the front of the greenhouse and looked it over carefully.

They spoke at the same time: "I've got a brilliant idea!"

They gave each other a Look. Kristy reached for her *Boss* hat.

She put it on Claudia's head.

With Claudia in charge, the BSC went to work. Dawn cleared branches and debris. Mallory scrubbed brick walls. Logan and Alan bailed out the flood. Mary Anne and Kristy repaired the BSC banner.

Claudia brought cans of paint from camp. She painted a mural over one of the walls. Inside, Alan and Logan put their handprints on the wall, slowly transforming Cokie's mess into a colorful pattern.

When everything was done, Kristy and her group hung the banner. Once again, the greenhouse was the proud future home of the Baby-sitters Club.

As campers began to arrive at the Spiers', Mary Anne shepherded them to the greenhouse.

Soon three cars drove past Mrs. Haberman's

house. From her porch, she watched them closely. Then her eyes darted to the greenhouse. She could see the members of the Baby-sitters Club waiting nervously.

The cars parked in front of the greenhouse. Out stepped three members of the Stoney-brook Civic Committee — Harold Weaver, Sheila Taub, and Louise Vanness. They were dressed in business suits, and from the expressions on their faces, they would have preferred to be in an air-conditioned office.

Off to the side, Logan and Alan were tossing rubber balls around with the campers, to keep them out of the way during the upcoming inspection.

Next to the greenhouse, unseen by the BSC, Cokie and her pals were climbing the old, leafy tree. "I've waited for this since first grade," Cokie grunted. "And I'm going to enjoy every minute of it."

As she inched out onto a thick branch, Cokie spotted the greenhouse for the first time since the night before. Her eyes widened. "Who do they know, Houdini?" she said under her breath.

The committee members greeted the girls in the BSC briefly, then headed inside to begin.

Jessi tried not to stare at the committee members. "Do they like it?" she asked.

Mallory shrugged. "Can't tell."

The inspection seemed to drag on forever. The committee members scribbled on legal pads and mumbled to each other. Their faces remained totally blank.

Finally, Mr. Weaver turned to the girls. "First," he began, "I'd like to say that we are very, very impressed by all your hard work."

Ms. Taub smiled. "You've shown a lot of civic pride."

"And we would love to grant your request to use the structure," Ms. Vanness went on, "but I'm afraid it's not possible."

Kristy felt as if she'd been hit by a truck. "Why?"

"You charge for your services, girls, don't you?" Mr. Weaver asked.

"Definitely," Claudia replied.

"So you would consider yourselves a money-making business, not a club?"

"Absolutely," Stacey agreed.

"Then I believe we have a problem here," Ms. Taub said. "Our charter says that any facility we oversee can be used only for non-profit organizations."

The BSC members stood there numbly, faces pale with shock.

"Excuse me, Sheila!" Mrs. Haberman's voice called out.

Everyone turned. Through the door, they

watched Mrs. Haberman walking briskly toward them, her chin set defiantly.

"Bird Face is on the committee?" Jessi whispered to Kristy. "We're dead."

"We're not talking about a multimillion-dollar corporation here," was the first thing Mrs. Haberman said to Ms. Taub. "They've done the work. Let's be fair."

"Emily!" Ms. Taub said with uneasy politeness. "Glad you could make it."

Ms. Vanness spoke up. "It's very hot in here. I'll meet you outside."

"Look, girls," Mr. Weaver continued, "Stoneybrook is indebted to you. And to show our gratitude, we would like to hang a commemorative plaque on the — "

"Get off it, Harold," Mrs. Haberman snapped. "You know perfectly well that these young women deserve the right to use this structure. I mean, how much could their business possibly make?"

"I don't know." Ms. Taub turned to the girls. "How much did you make this summer?"

"Well," Stacey began, "our expenses ran a little away from us. Between the start-up costs, freebies, supplies, fix-up money, and miscellaneous expenses, our total profit is . . ." She paused, adding in her head. "One hundred sixty-eight dollars and seventeen cents."

"That's all?" Mr. Weaver asked.

"I've got to get out of here," Ms. Taub muttered, heading for the door. "I can't breathe."

"They're dropping like flies," Jessi whispered in Mallory's ear.

"If my memory serves me, Harold," Mrs. Haberman said, "according to the committee bylaws, a company must show a profit of at least fifteen hundred dollars a year to qualify as a viable business. Therefore I see no reason why these girls can't use this as their office. They worked hard for it. They deserve it."

Mr. Weaver's eyes darted left and right. The other committee members were nowhere in sight. Beads of sweat rolled down her forehead. "Uh, fine, Emily. It's theirs. I — I need some air."

With a brief nod to the girls, Mr. Weaver left.

A smile crept across Mrs. Haberman's face. "I guess they're not used to such a tropical environment."

If Kristy hadn't had more self-control, she would have kissed her.

Outside, the tall, overhanging tree branch rustled. No one took much note of it. Anyone who had looked up would have spotted Cokie creeping further out, trying to find a better vantage point.

The committee members had stopped to watch the campers play ball. The girls in the BSC chatted away excitedly.

Kristy saw Jackie pick up a shovel and hold it like a bat. A few feet away, Matt wound up to pitch. Kristy chuckled to herself. This she had to see.

Matt lobbed the ball. Jackie let loose a wild swing.

Thwock!

He connected solidly. Kristy watched the ball shoot upward, into the tree. Her eyes were wide with surprise.

But not as wide as Cokie's.

"Who-o-oa!" Cokie cried. She let go of the branch to shield herself from the ball.

She caught the line drive — and fell backward out of the tree. Screaming, she landed in an open Dumpster.

When she hoisted herself out, her face was gray with soot and her hair was coated with debris.

Alan burst out laughing. One by one, Kristy and her friends joined him. Then Mrs. Haberman. Then, finally, the other members of the Stoneybrook Civic Committee.

Kristy ran to Jackie and gave him a high five.

"Hey, Dawn," Alan said, "want to go to the movies tonight?"

Dawn rolled her eyes. "Alan, get real."

"I am," Alan insisted. "I've been trying to ask you all summer."

Dawn gave him a hard look. Then she shrugged. "Okay."

Alan looked as if he would float away.

CHAPTER 22

Kristy felt sad the morning the BSC members began packing up the club paraphernalia in Claudia's room. Even though the greenhouse would be a fantastic new headquarters, it was tough to say good-bye to all the memories.

Claudia bustled in, carrying a tray of iced tea and cookies. "Room service!"

As she set it down, everyone dug in.

"Are we taking the bed, Claudia?" Mallory asked.

Claudia shook her head. "We can't take my furniture."

"What are we going to sit on?" Jessi asked.

"Can we take the carpet?" Mallory said.

Claudia gave her a Look. "Uh, Jessi, could you pass me the licorice from the nightstand? I don't want to forget it."

Jessi opened the drawer. She took out bags of candy and threw them to Claudia.

"I'm going to miss it here," Mary Anne said with a sigh.

"Remember this stain?" Mallory asked, pointing to the carpet.

Jessi laughed. "Yeah, when Claudia tried to make a triple chocolate marshmallow sundae look like the Empire State Building."

"That was the Eiffel Tower," Claudia corrected her.

"We spent most of the best years of our lives in this place," Mary Anne said.

For a long moment, no one responded.

"Come on, you guys," Kristy finally said. "Everything will work out. All we have to do is carry all this downstairs — " She gestured toward the piles of boxes.

"Get it outside somehow — " Stacey continued.

"Find something to sit on — " Jessi added.

"And bring a lot of water," Dawn said, "because we'll really need it in that place."

Stacey sat on the bed. "It's so nice and cool in here."

Kristy's mind was racing. Camp was to begin in an hour, and she had a great idea for a project.

A few hours later, the girls in the Baby-sitters Club, Alan and Logan, and their campers trudged up Burnt Hill Road, pulling red wagons. In the wagons were saplings, small potted flowers and seedlings, and huge sunflowers in planter boxes.

They turned up Mrs. Haberman's walkway. Dawn climbed her steps and rang the bell.

When the door opened, Mrs. Haberman stared at them in confusion.

"Sorry to bother you, Mrs. Haberman," Dawn said, "but there's something you've got to see."

She turned and gestured for Mrs. Haberman to follow. Wordlessly, they all walked down the street.

They stopped in front of the greenhouse. "It's all yours," Dawn said firmly.

Mrs. Haberman's jaw opened, but no words came out.

"We thought you could use it to grow all your flowers and stuff," Kristy added, nodding toward the wagons.

"We asked the man at the nursery for whatever might attract hummingbirds and butterflies." Dawn smiled proudly. "The sunflowers were my idea."

"Well, Stoneybrook could use a nature conservancy." As Mrs. Haberman laughed, her eyes brimmed with tears. "You guys might get your names on a plaque after all."

Until that moment, Kristy never thought she'd live to see Mrs. Haberman cry.

EPILOGUE

"Okay, everyone," Mrs. Haberman shouted. "Group shot! Come on."

The BSC Summer Camp crowded onto the greenhouse steps, which had six permanent indentations, after Cokie's and her friends' shoes had been removed.

Kristy elbowed her way front and center, making sure her *Boss* cap was facing the camera.

She was thinking about money. After buying the plants and an answering machine, the BSC had had eighteen dollars left over.

An entire summer's profit. Eighteen bucks.

So much for my big money ideas, Kristy thought.

But she tried to look on the bright side. That would be enough for a decent pizza party.

Around her, everyone jockeyed for position, laughing, cracking jokes, making faces. For the first time in weeks, Kristy felt like herself again. Boy, was that a nice feeling.

She still missed her dad, maybe even more than before. But at least she knew him. That was a start.

Maybe even more important, the Baby-sitters Club had survived. The friendships may have been battered a bit, but they were still there.

"Okay, everybody lean in and say, 'Trees'!" Mrs. Haberman called.

"TREEEEEEEEEES!"

Mrs. Haberman clicked the shutter, and everyone in the BSC collapsed with laughter.

In the midst of it all, Kristy remembered a saying her mom had once told her: If you can count the number of your friends on one hand, that's a lot.

Kristy felt very, very lucky. She was way ahead.

by Ann M. Martin

❏ MG43388-1	#1	Kristy's Great Idea	$3.50
❏ MG43387-3	#10	Logan Likes Mary Anne!	$3.50
❏ MG43717-8	#15	Little Miss Stoneybrook...and Dawn	$3.50
❏ MG43722-4	#20	Kristy and the Walking Disaster	$3.50
❏ MG43347-4	#25	Mary Anne and the Search for Tigger	$3.50
❏ MG42498-X	#30	Mary Anne and the Great Romance	$3.50
❏ MG42497-1	#31	Dawn's Wicked Stepsister	$3.50
❏ MG42496-3	#32	Kristy and the Secret of Susan	$3.50
❏ MG42495-5	#33	Claudia and the Great Search	$3.25
❏ MG42494-7	#34	Mary Anne and Too Many Boys	$3.50
❏ MG42508-0	#35	Stacey and the Mystery of Stoneybrook	$3.50
❏ MG43565-5	#36	Jessi's Baby-sitter	$3.50
❏ MG43566-3	#37	Dawn and the Older Boy	$3.25
❏ MG43567-1	#38	Kristy's Mystery Admirer	$3.25
❏ MG43568-X	#39	Poor Mallory!	$3.25
❏ MG44082-9	#40	Claudia and the Middle School Mystery	$3.25
❏ MG43570-1	#41	Mary Anne Versus Logan	$3.50
❏ MG44083-7	#42	Jessi and the Dance School Phantom	$3.50
❏ MG43572-8	#43	Stacey's Emergency	$3.50
❏ MG43573-6	#44	Dawn and the Big Sleepover	$3.50
❏ MG43574-4	#45	Kristy and the Baby Parade	$3.50
❏ MG43569-8	#46	Mary Anne Misses Logan	$3.50
❏ MG44971-0	#47	Mallory on Strike	$3.50
❏ MG43571-X	#48	Jessi's Wish	$3.50
❏ MG44970-2	#49	Claudia and the Genius of Elm Street	$3.25
❏ MG44969-9	#50	Dawn's Big Date	$3.50
❏ MG44968-0	#51	Stacey's Ex-Best Friend	$3.50
❏ MG44966-4	#52	Mary Anne + 2 Many Babies	$3.50
❏ MG44967-2	#53	Kristy for President	$3.25
❏ MG44965-6	#54	Mallory and the Dream Horse	$3.25
❏ MG44964-8	#55	Jessi's Gold Medal	$3.25
❏ MG45657-1	#56	Keep Out, Claudia!	$3.50
❏ MG45658-X	#57	Dawn Saves the Planet	$3.50

More titles... ➤

The Baby-sitters Club titles continued...

❏ MG45659-8 **#58 Stacey's Choice** $3.50
❏ MG45660-1 **#59 Mallory Hates Boys (and Gym)** $3.50
❏ MG45662-8 **#60 Mary Anne's Makeover** $3.50
❏ MG45663-6 **#61 Jessi's and the Awful Secret** $3.50
❏ MG45664-4 **#62 Kristy and the Worst Kid Ever** $3.50
❏ MG45665-2 **#63 Claudia's ~~Freind~~ Friend** $3.50
❏ MG45666-0 **#64 Dawn's Family Feud** $3.50
❏ MG45667-9 **#65 Stacey's Big Crush** $3.50
❏ MG47004-3 **#66 Maid Mary Anne** $3.50
❏ MG47005-1 **#67 Dawn's Big Move** $3.50
❏ MG47006-X **#68 Jessi and the Bad Baby-Sitter** $3.50
❏ MG47007-8 **#69 Get Well Soon, Mallory!** $3.50
❏ MG47008-6 **#70 Stacey and the Cheerleaders** $3.50
❏ MG47009-4 **#71 Claudia and the Perfect Boy** $3.50
❏ MG47010-8 **#72 Dawn and the We Love Kids Club** $3.50
❏ MG45575-3 **Logan's Story Special Edition Readers' Request** $3.25
❏ MG47118-X **Logan Bruno, Boy Baby-sitter**
Special Edition Readers' Request $3.50
❏ MG44240-6 **Baby-sitters on Board! Super Special #1** $3.95
❏ MG44239-2 **Baby-sitters' Summer Vacation Super Special #2** $3.95
❏ MG43973-1 **Baby-sitters' Winter Vacation Super Special #3** $3.95
❏ MG42493-9 **Baby-sitters' Island Adventure Super Special #4** $3.95
❏ MG43575-2 **California Girls! Super Special #5** $3.95
❏ MG43576-0 **New York, New York! Super Special #6** $3.95
❏ MG44963-X **Snowbound Super Special #7** $3.95
❏ MG44962-X **Baby-sitters at Shadow Lake Super Special #8** $3.95
❏ MG45661-X **Starring the Baby-sitters Club Super Special #9** $3.95
❏ MG45674-1 **Sea City, Here We Come! Super Special #10** $3.95

Available wherever you buy books...or use this order form.

Scholastic Inc., P.O. Box 7502, 2931 E. McCarty Street, Jefferson City, MO 65102

Please send me the books I have checked above. I am enclosing $_____
(please add $2.00 to cover shipping and handling). Send check or money order - no
cash or C.O.D.s please.

Name _____ Birthdate_____

Address _____

City_____ State/Zip_____

Please allow four to six weeks for delivery. Offer good in the U.S. only. Sorry, mail orders are not
available to residents of Canada. Prices subject to change.

BSC993

Hey BSC Fans—Look What's Coming Soon!

Kristy, Dawn, and Stacey have a brand-new look...and they're better than ever!

Every book is now jam-packed with plenty of NEW stuff:

✿ Colorful new covers
✿ Fabulous scrapbook starring each book's narrator
✿ Fill-in pages so you can personalize your copy
✿ Special note from author Ann M. Martin
✿ All-new fan club offer in the back of every book

Don't miss out...Collect 'em all!

Look for the first-to-be-released, ALL-NEW and updated The Baby-sitters Club books #1 through #5—available at bookstores everywhere this September.

BSCC295

Now **THE BABY-SITTERS CLUB®**

★ **is a Video Club too!** ★

JOIN TODAY—

- Save $5.00 on your first video!
- 10-day FREE examination-before-you-keep policy!
- New video adventure every other month!
- Never an obligation to buy anything!

Now you can play back the adventures of America's favorite girls whenever you like. Share them with your friends too.

Just pop a tape into a VCR and watch *Claudia and the Mystery of the Secret Passage* or view *Mary Anne and the Brunettes, The Baby-sitters and the Boy Sitters, Dawn Saves the Trees* or any of the girls' many exciting, fun-packed adventures.

Don't miss this chance to actually see and hear Kristy, Stacey, Mallory, Jessi and the others in this new video series. Full details below.

■■■ ■■■ ■■■ CUT OUT AND MAIL TODAY! ■■■ ■ ■■

MAIL TO: Baby-sitters Video Club • P.O. Box 30628 • Tampa, FL 33630-0628

Please enroll me as a member of the Baby-sitters Video Club and send me the first video, *Mary Anne and the Brunettes* for only $9.95 plus $2.50 shipping and handling. I will then receive other video adventures—one approximately every other month—at the regular price of $14.95 plus $2.50 shipping/handling each for a 10-day FREE examination. There is never any obligation to buy anything.

NAME	PLEASE PRINT
ADDRESS	APT.
CITY	
STATE	ZIP
BIRTH DATE	
( ) AREA CODE	DAYTIME PHONE NUMBER

CHECK ONE:
- ☐ I enclose $9.95 plus $2.50 shipping/handling.
- ☐ Charge to my card: ☐ VISA ☐ MASTERCARD ☐ AMEX

Card number_____ Expiration Date_____

Parent's signature:_____ 9AP S5

Wow! It's really them— the new Baby-sitters Club dolls!

Your favorite Baby-sitters Club characters have come to life in these beautiful collector dolls. Each doll wears her own unique clothes and jewelry. They look just like the girls you have imagined! The dolls also come with their own individual stories in special edition booklets that you'll find nowhere else.

Look for the new Baby-sitters Club collection... coming soon to a store near you!

Kenner®

The Baby-sitters Club © 1994 Scholastic, Inc. All Rights Reserved. ®* Kenner, a Division of Tonka Corporation Cincinnati, Ohio 45202

The purchase of this item will result in a donation to the Ann M. Martin Foundation, dedicated to benefiting children, education and literacy programs, and the homeless.